What Will Become of the Children?

Studies in German Literature, Linguistics, and Culture

CLAIRE BERGMANN

WHAT WILL BECOME OF THE CHILDREN?

A NOVEL OF A GERMAN FAMILY IN
THE TWILIGHT OF WEIMAR BERLIN

Translated and with an introduction by
Richard Bodek

 CAMDEN HOUSE
Rochester, New York

First published 2010 by Camden House

Camden House is an imprint of Boydell & Brewer Inc.
668 Mt. Hope Avenue, Rochester, NY 14620, USA
www.camden-house.com
and of Boydell & Brewer Limited
PO Box 9, Woodbridge, Suffolk IP12 3DF, UK
www.boydellandbrewer.com

Hardback ISBN-13: 978-1-57113-466-0
Hardback ISBN-10: 1-57113-466-2
Paperback ISBN-13: 978-1-57113-464-6
Paperback ISBN-10: 1-57113-464-6

Library of Congress Cataloging-in-Publication Data

Bergmann, Claire, b. 1898.
    [Was wird aus deinen kindern, Pitt?. English]
    What will become of the children? : a novel of a German family in the
twilight of Weimar Berlin / Claire Bergmann; translated and with an
introduction by Richard Bodek.
        p. cm. — (Studies in German literature, linguistics, and culture)
        Originally published as Was wird aus deinen kindern, Pitt? in 1932.
        Includes bibliographical references.
    ISBN-13: 978-1-57113-466-0 (hardback: alk. paper)
    ISBN-10: 1-57113-466-2 (hardback: alk. paper)
    ISBN-13: 978-1-57113-464-6 (pbk.: alk. paper)
    ISBN-10: 1-57113-464-6 (pbk.: alk. paper)
        1. Families—Germany—Fiction. 2. Germany—Social conditions
—1918–1933—Fiction. 3. Germany—History—1918–1933—Fiction.
4. Berlin (Germany)—Fiction.   I. Bodek, Richard, 1961–   II. Title.
III. Series.

PT2603.E627W313 2010
833'.912--dc22

                                                              2010017183

A catalogue record for this title is available from the British Library.

This publication is printed on acid-free paper.
Printed in the United States of America.

CONTENTS

ACKNOWLEDGMENTS

A NUMBER OF PEOPLE, in very different ways, made the translation and publication of this book possible.

Michael Brenner of the University of Munich, who obtained a copy of the book for me, without which this project would have ended before it even began.

The interlibrary loan staff at the College of Charleston (Anita Calderon, Ann Cotton, Shirley Davidson, Beverly Gumb, Chris Nelson, and Michael Phillips), who were remarkable in getting German sources that helped to contextualize the novel.

Tom Baginski, Jason Coy, Cara Delay, Steven Della Lana, Bryan Ganaway, James Hardin, Anton Kaes, David Kettler, Gerhard Mack, and Nancy Nenno, who all helped with some tricky translations.

Tim Carens and Scott Peeples of the English Department at the College of Charleston, both of whom listened to me talk about this translation and offered more ideas on how to make it successful than could be expected of any reasonable person.

Cynthia Lowenthal, Dean of Humanities and Social Sciences at the College of Charleston, who encouraged me to put other research projects on hold and focus on this even when there was no guarantee of publication.

Jim Walker, my editor at Camden House, who supported all stages of the project and fine-tuned the translation, making it far better than it would otherwise have been.

The Research and Development Committee of the College of Charleston, which provided a generous grant to help fund this translation.

Finally, my deepest gratitude goes to Amy Shore, the first person to read *What Will Become of the Children?* in English. She always reminded me that the translation and publication of this novel represented a posthumous victory of the Weimar Spirit.

INTRODUCTION

SOMETIME DURING AUTUMN 1932, Claire Bergmann's novel, *Was wird aus deinen Kindern, Pitt?* appeared in German bookstores. It is fair to say that it enjoyed an immediate, mostly positive critical reception. It is also fair to say that it has fallen into almost complete obscurity. As we will soon see, this work chronicles the travails of the Deutsch family from its rise in the 1890s until the summer of 1932. At the onset, the central character is Pitt Deutsch, a traditional conservative, and, as his name implies, a kind of German Everyman. Loyal to the Kaiser, Deutsch rises from skilled worker to wartime millionaire, and then loses everything in the postwar hyperinflation. The rest of the book is set in 1932 (mostly in Berlin) and switches its focus to the Deutsch children. Two are out-of-work academics. Two are Nazis. Two are secretaries and one is a "kept woman." Among the book's subplots and themes are a German-Jewish romance, the appearance and trials of the "New Woman," the psychological costs of unemployment, Nazi-Communist street violence, Nazi harassment of Jews, and abortion. It also makes reference to the year's many national elections, the Lausanne Conference, and other contemporary political events. The quickening politics of the late Weimar Republic and the Nazi accession to power overtook the book's contemporary message, and its relevance waned, until the work resurfaced, in a sense, when it appeared on the 1938 *Liste des schädlichen und unerwünschten Schrifttums,* the list of books banned in Germany during the Third Reich.[1]

My discovery of this book was a happy accident. I was reading a microfilmed edition of the *Vossische Zeitung,* one of Weimar Berlin's newspapers of record, for a long-term research project when I stumbled across a review of the work by Hans Fallada.[2] For some reason, perhaps because I admire Fallada's classic novel, *Kleiner Mann, was nun?* (What Now, Little Man?), I read and was fascinated by his praise for a novel about then current events, and made a note of it for later reading. Imagine my surprise when, according to WorldCat, fewer than a dozen libraries in the world had this book. Un-

---

[1] This list can be accessed at http://www.berlin.de/rubrik/hauptstadt/verbannte_buecher/detail.php?referer=%2Frubrik%2Fhauptstadt%2Fverbannte_buecher%2Fsuche.php&id=70655&page=0&suche=bergmann&amp.

[2] Hans Fallada, "Familie Deutsch/ein Alltags-Roman von heute," *Vossische Zeitung,* 23 October 1932 (morning).

able to access it through interlibrary loan, I was fortunate enough to have a friend, Professor Michael Brenner of the University of Munich, who was gracious enough to make a photocopy of the text and send it across the Atlantic.

You can imagine my pleasant surprise when I opened the copy to find a sensitive novel about middle-class life during the Depression, one of the best portraits of Berlin on the eve of the Third Reich I have ever read, made all the more interesting by the fact that the author did not see the Third Reich as imminent. After a little more exploration I found two other contemporary reviews, one positive, one not, all of which convinced me that this work deserves a new, wider audience.[3] The author, Claire Bergmann, is even more mysterious than the work. I found one brief reference to her in a multi-volume lexicon of German literature of the twentieth century, listing only a birth date (October 27, 1898) and the Berlin city district in which she lived.[4] The Berlin address books list a Claire Bergmann — journalist — as residing in the city from 1932 to 1934, after which she simply vanishes.[5] Inquiries to literary archives in Germany, indeed even a letter to the editor in the *Times Literary Supplement* putting out a call for any information on Bergmann failed to find anything more. For better or worse, then, the book will have to speak for itself. The rest of this introduction provides a very brief history of the Weimar Republic, and then sketches the Berlin of 1932, the work's central stage.

A Brief History of the Weimar Republic

In order to understand the book more completely, we should take a brief look at the history of the Germany within which it takes place. The novel begins in the waning days of Germany's Kaiserreich, or empire. From the 1890s until 1913, Germany appeared, on the surface, to be a wealthy, stable, and progressive country, one that might well be predicted to lead Europe into a bright twentieth century. Underneath this surface, however, lay a

---

[3] Siegfried Krakauer's positive review appeared in the *Frankfurter Zeitung* on 16 February 1933, and can be found at www.angestellten.de/rezensionen/rez._bergmann01.html. The other review, which appeared in the *Berliner Tageblatt* on 20 November 1932, was signed only "Gertrud," and was negative because she believed that Bergmann's work read more like reportage than fiction.

[4] W.K., Listing for Claire Bergmann in Konrad Feilchenfeldt, ed., *Deutsches Literatur-Lexikon das 20. Jahrhundert* (K. G. Saur Verlag, Bern and Munich, 2001) vol. 2, 392.

[5] Berlin's address books from 1799 until 1943 can be accessed at the website of the Zentral und Landesbibliothek Berlin (http://adressbuch.zlb.de/).

series of problems that struck at the empire's core. Internationally, Germany found itself desiring to be a world power, able to compete with Great Britain on the global stage. In the process of trying to make this possible, however, it managed to alienate not only Britain, but two of Europe's other major powers: France and Russia. This was an alarming development on a continent with only one other power with which to ally, namely Austria. Internally, Germany's social structure led to mounting class conflict between a growing working-class movement and conservative forces that wanted to maintain their grip on power. The combination of external friction and internal tension led the government into a series of international crises, all of which culminated in a continental, then world war. This war, which began in August 1914, dragged on, finally culminating in an unforeseen disaster — Germany's defeat, the monarchy's collapse, and its replacement by the Weimar Republic.

At its birth, the Weimar Republic was unexpected, unwanted, and unloved. When Germany entered the First World War in 1914, most of its subjects believed that the conflict would end by Christmas with German soldiers celebrating victory in Paris. Instead, four grueling, bloody, hungry years ensued, at the end of which Germans, who had been told by their government that they were winning, had to deal with a stunning defeat, which in turn led to a number of previously unimaginable twists and turns. Sailors mutinied in the city of Kiel on the Baltic, radicals declared a republic in Bavaria, and Workers' and Soldiers' Councils (or soviets) formed across the country's industrial regions. These dramatic events formed the backdrop to parliamentary reform and parliamentary government, instituted in October 1918 and culminating on November 9, when Kaiser Wilhelm II abdicated. Through a series of rather complicated maneuvers, Germany's nascent constitutional monarchy quickly became a republic under the direction of Friedrich Ebert, a moderate socialist and leader of Germany's Social Democratic Party, whose governmental ideal was Great Britain.

Even as this was happening, a more radical left came under the guidance of Rosa Luxemburg and Karl Liebknecht. Luxemburg, perhaps the most interesting revolutionary theorist of her time, believed that the SPD had abandoned its goal of Marxist revolution for a lukewarm progressivism. Liebknecht, a lawyer and member of the Reichstag, had become a revolutionary critic of the war. Their disgust with the republic's incrementalism culminated in revolutionary action on January 5 and 6, 1919, when the nascent Communist Party made a serious attempt to wrest power from the new government. Luxemburg found this to be a misguided effort, not believing that such a revolutionary action could either be successful, or could culminate in the fundamental social changes that she supported. Nevertheless, she felt obligated to support her Communist comrades who wanted to emulate Russia's successful Bolshevik revolution.

The central government, with the help of right-wing paramilitary forces, crushed the uprising within a week, murdering Luxemburg and Liebknecht in the process. This bloody action destroyed the chances of any far-reaching social and political change and killed any chance of socialist unity in the coming years, indeed, it could be seen as the beginning of a fratricidal enmity in the German left. Over the course of the republic's history, both the Communists and the Socialists would view each other as little better than the Nazis. At one point, after 1928, the Communists would even refer to the SPD as a party of "Social Fascists."

Even in the midst of this revolutionary activity, the process of building a government progressed. Elections to the new National Assembly went forward on January 19, 1919, returning a majority of delegates from parties committed to making Germany a successful parliamentary democracy. Within a year the country had a new constitution that guaranteed proportional representation, a directly elected president, and federalism. It also had the soon-to-be infamous Article 48 of its constitution, which allowed the president, in times of extraordinary danger to the republic, to take emergency action without the agreement of the parliament. At the republic's end, the extraordinary would become ordinary, and the use of this power the norm.

Even in its early days, though, the republic faced a series of crises. The first of these was the Versailles Treaty ending the war. Most Germans expected their treatment to be relatively benign under Woodrow Wilson's famous Fourteen Points, which were introduced in a speech that contained these lines:

> We have no jealousy of German greatness, and there is nothing in this program that impairs it. We grudge her no achievement or distinction of learning or of pacific enterprise such as have made her record very bright and very enviable. We do not wish to injure her or to block in any way her legitimate influence or power. We do not wish to fight her either with arms or with hostile arrangements of trade, if she is willing to associate herself with us and the other peace-loving nations of the world in covenants of justice and law and fair dealing.
>
> We wish her only to accept a place of equality among the peoples of the world — the new world in which we now live — instead of a place of mastery.

They were thus horrified with the treaty presented to their government the following spring. In this Versailles Treaty, the negotiations from which the German delegation was barred, Germany was forced to cede a significant amount of territory to a newly reconstituted Poland, as well as to France, Lithuania, and Denmark. Germany lost all of its colonial possessions, saw its armed forces reduced to 100,000 officers and men, and was required to pay billions of gold marks in reparations. Perhaps most aggravating to Germans was Article 231, the so-called war-guilt clause:

> The Allied and Associated Governments affirm and Germany accepts the responsibility of Germany and her allies for causing all the loss and damage to which the Allied and Associated Governments and their nationals have been subjected as a consequence of the war imposed upon them by the aggression of Germany and her allies.

Many later observers believed that the Treaty of Versailles doomed Weimar from the start. That assessment is greatly overstated. Nevertheless, there is no question that the republic's legitimacy was immediately an issue for many, especially those on the right. Weimar's early crises were not, however, restricted to left-wing agitation and political issues. Three other crises defined the republic's early years: the Kapp Putsch, runaway inflation, and the Ruhr Crisis.

In March, 1920, a right-wing camarilla under the leadership of Wolfgang Kapp, an obscure civil servant, tried to seize power in Berlin. Although the putsch failed in less than a week, the causes of its failures gave pause. It was not put down by the army, which remained in its barracks, but rather by a general strike. The legitimate, democratically elected, government could not count on the loyalty of its own military, but needed the support of labor. Germany's inflation began in 1914 when it decided to pay for the war by printing currency rather than through raising taxes. The government's assumption was that the war's cost would be recouped from reparations payments by the losers. The inflationary spiral did not stop, however, and by 1923, the US Dollar (worth 4 to 5 marks in 1913) was valued at 1 trillion marks. This wiped out the life savings of many average Germans who had spent their lives working hard and saving. Even as the inflation was proceeding apace, French and Belgian military forces occupied the Ruhr to push Germany into fulfilling its reparations agreements. The local policy of passive resistance, which amounted to doing no work that would help the occupiers, further stoked the hyperinflation. Also in 1923, perhaps the worst year in the early years of the Republic, Adolf Hitler and his nascent National Socialist (Nazi) Party attempted to overthrow the Republic. Their hope was to occupy Munich and then march on Berlin in a move reminiscent of Mussolini's March on Rome in the autumn of 1922. In what might be described as a comedy of errors, they never even succeeded in taking power in Munich. Although this coup attempt, like the Kapp Putsch before it, failed quite quickly, it and the subsequent trial of its leader vaulted Hitler and his movement to fame in Germany.

By 1924, though, political crises had been averted, the inflation had been brought under control, France seems to have understood that it stood virtually alone in its attempt to punish Germany as harshly as possible, and the republic entered its second phase, a relatively stable period in which the economy seemed to have righted itself, politics took on a more normal appearance, and Germany — or at least its capital, Berlin — entered the so-called "Golden Twenties."

The Republic's Middle Years

Just as Tolstoy reminds us that happy families are alike, but unhappy families are unhappy in their own ways, it is almost fair to say that the middle years of the Weimar Republic, at least politically, were politically much like the quiet years in other countries, and not of any particular interest. Unemployment, compared to what would happen during the Great Depression, was low, only going above 10% once in the stable years of the mid 1920s.[6] And prices were stable. Nevertheless, parliaments were rather fractious and unruly; cabinets did not last very long, and Paul von Hindenburg (Weimar's second and last elected president, serving from 1925 until 1933) sought greater consensus among politicians. Germany's foreign policy, under the able leadership of short-term Chancellor (August-November, 1923) and long-time Foreign Minister Gustav Stresemann, brought it back into the world of European politics.[7] In the Locarno Pact of 1925, for example, Germany recognized its western borders with France as legitimate and agreed that any revisions of its eastern borders would be done peacefully. It was also in these few years that the Dawes Plan, which reduced Germany's reparations burden, was implemented and that Germany joined the League of Nations. These are the years often referred to as the Golden Twenties because of the glittering surface of Weimar Culture. Fascinating as this culture is, and as much as it resonates for us in such vehicles as the Broadway musical and later film, *Cabaret* and the works of luminaries such as Erwin Piscator, George Grosz, and Arnold Schoenberg (Austrian by birth, but a giant on Berlin's classical musical scene), it is worth remembering that this culture only appealed to a fairly narrow range of Germans. For most of the population a popular culture consisting of easily forgotten songs and ephemeral films trumped the avant-garde.

During the Weimar years, Berlin loomed large on the German horizon, culturally, economically, and demographically. In 1925, the city had a popu-

[6] Table B2, "Unemployment," *International Historical Statistics Europe 1750–1988* (New York: Stockton Press, 1992), 160.

[7] As Chancellor, Stresemann was instrumental in ending France's occupation and Germany's hyperinflation, but his apparent capitulation to France to effect this made him unacceptable to Germany's right, and ended his ability to hold onto the top cabinet position.

lation of 4,000,000.[8] Although today, perhaps because of the popularity of singers such as Ute Lemper, frequent revivals of Bertolt Brecht and Kurt Weill's *The Threepenny Opera,* and the nostalgia for German expressionist film and art, this is thought of as a golden time, we ought to remember that Berlin North, where the Deutsch family lived, was a maze of streets, each resembling the others, with a series of shops, bakeries, bars, butchers, tobacconists, and barbershops. Trash overflowed onto the sidewalks. Pedestrians were immersed in the sounds of taxis, trams, playing children, drunks, and gramophones playing the latest hits, as well as the acrid odor of the brown coal that heated furnaces and stoves and powered the city's industry. One might find shoppers like Klara Deutsch going to a local market, where items as diverse as suspenders, smoked herring, shoe leather, wine grapes, slippers, wreaths, cook pots, and Bockwursts were sold. Shoppers circled the hall several times to find the best prices, a necessity in the depths of the depression.[9]

Politically, the relatively stable middle 1920s could be said to have lasted from 1924 until 1929. Their stability is only relative compared to the years that proceeded and followed them. One of the hallmarks of this era was the impossibility of building a ruling coalition that would stretch from the Social Democrats on the left to the German National Peoples Party on the right. In February 1925, Friedrich Ebert, the republic's first president, died. In the first round of the election campaign to choose his successor, candidates who supported democracy held a clear majority, but no one of them had enough votes to win the office. In the second round, the right chose a new candidate, Paul von Hindenburg, military hero of the First World War, and he was elected.

Under President von Hindenburg, Germany endured a series of fragile coalitions. The socio-political issues of the era revolved around labor relations and personal rights. It is not much of an exaggeration to say that the political situation boiled down to the organized left's attempt to hold onto the improvements in wages, working hours, and working conditions that it had gained during the revolution, and leftists and liberals demanding that women should have the right to control their own bodies, against a reactionary right that wanted to roll back the gains of the left, send women back

---

[8] Berthold Grzywatz, *Arbeit und Bevölkerung im Berlin der Weimarer Zeit: Eine historisch-statistische Untersuchung* (West Berlin, 1988), 29.

[9] Both this paragraph and some of the following description is adapted from my book, *Proletarian Performance in Weimar Berlin* (Columbia, SC: Camden House, 1997). On shopping in Wedding, see Fritz Köhler, "Notizen über den Wedding," *Die Rote Fahne,* 28 November 1928, and Willy Römer, *Ambulantes Gewerbe Berlin 1904–1932* (Berlin: Edition Photothek, 1983).

into very traditional roles, and water down, if not entirely eliminate, parliamentary government as a whole.

Election campaigns — which became ever more frequent toward the end of the Weimar Republic as parliamentary governments repeatedly fell — gave the city's streets a colorful, more political aspect. The Litfass poles — large cylindrical columns that served as slates upon which all sorts of notices could be posted — that pop up in the novel would be covered with posters urging voters to support the Nazis, Communists, Social Democrats, and a host of other parties.

Perhaps as a kind of diversion from Weimar's incessant electoral politics, we see in several places in Bergmann's novel that going to the movies was one of the most important leisure activities available to Berliners. Matinees were common; during the Depression, tickets cost forty to sixty pfennig, with a discount for the unemployed. A Count Stenbock-Fermor reported that along Berlin's Münzstrasse, cinemas were open from 10:00 A.M. to 1:00 A.M., that for sixty pfennig one could spend the entire day inside, and that they were always full. The programs were replete with violence, sensationalism and sex, lasted from three to four hours and were advertised with signs like the following:

Today the great, sensational and giant program!

From the Berlin Underworld (Cellar Cavaliers), 10 acts.

Fighting Against Bandits, 6 acts.

Tarzan and the Golden Lion, 8 acts.

Cultural Film.

or

Today 4 Hits!

Double Wedding with Obstacles, 7 acts.

The Train Robbers from Texas (The Pacific Railway), 10 acts.

The Family without Morals (A powerful picture about decency in 7 grandiose acts).

The Black Pierrot (8 breathtaking acts).[10]

---

[10] Graf Alexander Stenbock-Fermor, *Deutschland von Unten: Reise durch die proletarische Provinz* (Stuttgart: J. Engelhorn, 1931), 143–44.

Even a few hours at a cinema, however, would do little to alleviate the almost unremitting grimness of everyday life, life that would become increasingly harder as the republic neared its end.

Depression and the Crisis Year of 1932

On two days in October 1929, the New York Stock Exchange crashed and crashed again, leading to the longest and deepest economic depression in the history of the industrialized world. This, combined with the August 1929 adoption of the Young Plan, led to a series of circumstances that helped to doom democracy in Weimar Germany, and to the rise of the most radical of Germany's right-wing political parties, the NSDAP, or Nazi Party. The Young Plan, named after American banker Owen Young, was designed to reduce Germany's annual reparations payments by stretching them over fifty-nine years, and to continue Germany's reintegration into the world of international trade. In short, though, the so-called respectable right saw this as a further enslavement of Germany, and it began to look even worse after the full ramifications of the American crash began to be felt in Europe.

For a series of economic reasons more complicated than we can deal with here, the Depression struck Germany harder than it did the other industrialized nations. German unemployment, which hit 15.3% in 1930, peaked at 31% in 1932.[11] This, in turn, led to a political situation which made it almost impossible for stable coalitions to form that could govern Germany. Because of this parliamentary impasse, President von Hindenburg found himself able to choose his own chancellor and cabinets — men with a reactionary outlook on politics, German society, and Germany's "proper" place in the world — and thus rule through the use of Article 48 and modify or destroy many of the democratic and social democratic rights enjoyed by German citizens. This situation was aided by a series of parliamentary elections that failed to return workable majorities, resulting in the collapse of democratic institutions and parliamentary responsibility. As the Depression deepened and these "cabinets of barons" became increasingly unpopular, the Nazis and the Communist saw their support grow. The Nazi vote in Reichstag elections grew from 2.6% in 1928 to a high of 37.3% in the first election of 1932, making them the single largest party in the parliament, while Adolf Hitler captured 13.4 million votes in the second round of the 1932 presi-

---

[11] Table B2, "Unemployment" *International Historical Statistics Europe 1750–1988* (New York: Stockton Press, 1992), 163.

dential elections (against eventual winner von Hindenburg's 19.4 million).[12] It is important to emphasize that, as is apparent from a careful reading of *What Will Become of the Children?*, Germany's move away from democratic principles did not necessitate the rise of the Third Reich. A series of scandals and crises in 1932, however, made some sort of extreme outcome seem ever more likely. It is to 1932, most especially in Berlin, that we will now turn.

Berlin 1932

In the novel, the optimism that Max Deutsch, second-oldest of Pitt Deutsch's four sons, holds for the future of his family, city, and country in 1932 might have been admirable, but was unwarranted. Berlin witnessed a number of events in that year that brought smiles to observers of popular culture, but much of the political and social events would leave most shaking their heads in sadness and confusion.

University Life

Both Max and his older brother Peter Deutsch are university graduates. Max, in his student days, was even involved in some political activity. Nevertheless, as he remarks to his sister, university life had changed by 1932. Germany had 100,000 university students, a massive increase from 1911's 55,000.[13] Many, if not most, of these students were drawn to radical right-wing politics. Nazi student organizations began to challenge the traditional dueling societies for leadership on campus.[14] Even the *New York Times* found the Nazi attraction to students interesting enough to devote to it a two-page article.[15] Indeed, in the January election for the University of Berlin's Student Senate, the National Socialists drew 3,500 votes to a mere 850 for the older fraternities. Liberal observers could only comfort themselves by commenting that this represented a quarter of the university's 14,000 students, most of whom failed to vote.[16] When Adolf Hitler spoke to

[12] Tim Kirk, *The Longman Companion to Nazi Germany* (New York: Longman, 1995), table 4.1, Elections for the Reichstag During the Weimar Republic, p.22, and table 4.4 Presidential Elections, 1932, p. 23.

[13] Otto Benecke, "Akademisches Proletariat," *Berliner Tageblatt*, 15 January 1932 (evening).

[14] "SA oder Couleur?" *Vossische Zeitung*, 19 January 1932 (evening).

[15] Harold Callender, "To the Nazi Colors the Students Flock. Crowding the German Universities, They Are the Sons of the Middle class, to Whom Politics is the New Romance," *New York Times*, January 17, 1932.

[16] "Ruhe an der Universität: Nationalsozialistisches Täuschungs-manöver," *Vossische Zeitung*, 25 January 1932 (evening).

the university's students, he drew a crowd of 8,000.[17] Even more ominous were several riots that broke out on campus between Nazi and left-wing students.[18] On January 22, forty uniformed Nazi students shut the university down when they marched into the main hall, attacked Jewish students, and marched out singing the Nazi anthems "The Horst Wessel Song" and "Germany Awake, Juda die in misery!"[19]

Nazi students shut the university down again in February, June, and July, the last prompting one American exchange student to comment that he found it odd that Europeans felt that American students' lack of interest in politics was a form of psychological malady, as if such actions represented a healthy interest in politics.[20] Similar incidents of violence and university closings affected the universities in Halle, Hamburg, Frankfurt, and Breslau. One of the Nazi student leaders stated that the violence would not cease until all Jewish students were expelled.[21]

Diversions: The Occult, Sport, and Other Heroics

Perhaps, given the crisis of 1932, it should be no surprise that there was a real upswing in interest in those things which could divert, or at least moderate, interest in one's own immediate circumstances. Among these was occultism. There was a proliferation of astrologists claiming that they read people's futures not for the money but merely to help them. For a mere 50 pfennig one could learn one's fate in the year to come.[22] Scientists took such phenomena seriously enough to conduct experiments to test the claims.[23] For those who did not want to visit a psychic, books of magic and even

---

[17] O.H., "Das Weltanschauungsplakat: Hitler vor seinen Studenten," *Vossische Zeitung*, 18 January 1932 (evening).

[18] "Wieder Ausschreitungen an der Berliner Universität," *Berliner Tageblatt*, 21 January 1932 (evening).

[19] "Berliner Universität geschlossen," *Vossische Zeitung*, 22 January 1932 (evening); "Berliner Universität geschlossen," *Berliner Tageblatt*, 22 January 1932 (evening); "Der Krawall an der Universität. Die Schuld der Nationalsozialisten," *Berliner Tageblatt*, 23 January 1932 (morning).

[20] William T. Payne, "Wir in Amerika . . .," *Vossische Zeitung*, 24 July 1932 (morning).

[21] "Vor einer Dauerschliessung der Universität. Die Nationalsozialisten bekennen sich als Angreifer: Sie fordern Entfernung der jüdischen Studenten," *Berliner Tageblatt*, 1 July 1932 (morning).

[22] Emil Fürst, "Astrologe an der Bordschwelle: Ihr Schicksal — für fünfzig Pfennig," *Die Vossische Zeitung*, 4 January 1932.

[23] Dr. M., "Das Rollkommando beim Hellseher. Experimente in der Gesellschaft für wissenschaftliche Philosophie," *Berliner Tageblatt*, 8 June 1932 (evening).

magic powders were freely available.[24] Shops selling these occult supplies could also perform more mundane services in these desperate times. When a young woman showed up at such a shop to enquire about painless methods of suicide, the patron responded that she was too dumb to do it successfully: the stars showed that she would fail but become a cripple for life. He was then able to direct her to a homeless shelter, which took her in.[25]

Berliners' interest also extended to lighter matters, as can be seen in the interest that the city showered on the heroes of the day. Jimmy Mattern, renowned aviation pioneer, who flew to Berlin from Newfoundland in a mere nineteen hours was the toast of the city, as he tried to break the record for a round-the-world trip — although this excitement turned quickly to concern when his airplane disappeared over the Soviet Union, and relief when he and his navigator were found.[26]

Rudolf Caracciola and Manfred von Brauchitsch captured the attention of Berlin in the May 1932 running of the Berlin Grand Prix. 300,000 spectators lined the 10-kilometer course along the AVUS (a section of Berlin's roadway system designed to serve as an oval raceway). Von Brauchitsch won with a record speed of 194.4 kilometers per hour in his Mercedes Benz, just edging Caracciola in his Alfa Romeo. Such speeds were dangerous, but they appealed to the public's love of technology and the appearance of progress, the drivers themselves often cast in the role of pioneers of speed and modernity. As one contemporary observed, "Sport" needed to be seen as more than just a self-contained activity; it represented the spiritual fulfillment of the age. To ask the question "why auto racing?" would be "extremely stupid. One might just as easily ask why fly, why cycle, why sail, why smoke cigarettes, or why wear a shirt. In short, why have modern civilization and culture?"[27]

The same love of technology and progress might explain the 20,000 people who waited by a Berlin lake, the Müggelsee, to watch the Dornier Do X land. The Do X, in its day the world's largest airplane, had twelve motors, 6,000 horsepower, and could carry more than 160 people. The

---

[24] Olli, "Hausse in Propheten," *Berliner Tageblatt*, 23 March 1932.

[25] Olli, "Hausse in Propheten," *Berliner Tageblatt*, 23 March 1932.

[26] "Weltflieger in Berlin. Neufundland — Berlin in 19 Stünden," *Berliner Tageblatt*, 7 July 1932 (morning) and "Wo sind die Flieger?" *Berliner Tageblatt*, 8 July 1932 (morning) and "Bei Minsk notgelandet!" *Berliner Tageblatt*, 8 July 1932 (evening).

[27] "Todesrennen oder nicht? Die Rennen sind Vorläufer des Fortschritts, die Fahrer seine Pioniere," *Berliner Tageblatt*, 29 May 1932 (morning). For the winning speed, see the Continental tire advertisement in the *Berliner Tageblatt*, 24 May 1932 (morning). Continental was proud to have provided the tires for the first through fifth finishers.

event was held at the Müggelsee because the plane had to take off and land on water. The May 24th arrival would be the first in Berlin since the Do X practiced 318 takeoffs and landings there in September 1930.[28]

It might be argued that a love of technology bound together the fascination with "spiritual science," auto racing, and aviation. Interestingly, as we shall see, much of the crime of the era was also interwoven with modernity and technology.

Crime

Berliners with a taste for crime would have found 1932 to be an interesting year, as violence and sensation made their presence known. The year in crime began with a fight between two international thieves on a street corner. They seem to have had a falling-out when one came to believe that the other was having an affair with his wife, an actress. Ludwig Gerl, the jealous husband, an Austrian in Berlin on a stolen passport, pulled a knife on Alexander Arba, a Rumanian traveling on a Hungarian passport. Arba proceeded to shoot Gerl and disappear into the night with Vera Baltrack, Gerl's wife.[29]

More directly pertaining to *What Will Become of the Children?* was a series of crimes that spoke directly to some of the book's themes. Among them, unsurprisingly in a year of deep economic depression, was the wave of counterfeiting that struck the city. Perhaps the most peculiar of the cases was that of Dr. Kornell Salaban, who, with his wife, was arrested on suspicion of minting 30,000 counterfeit two-mark coins. According to the Salabans' own confessions, they would dress in ratty clothing and take the coins to local markets to spend on groceries, receiving real coins in change. Their case was peculiar for a number of reasons. Contemporary experts believed that the equipment and supplies necessary for such an operation would render it minimally profitable at best. Even odder was Dr. Salaban's double life. Like a real life Dr. Caligari or Dr. Mabuse, Salaban had a very respectable "day job," in his case as the publisher of *European Book of Attorneys and Notaries.* Indeed, in the wake of his arrest, investigators could find no trace of his claimed law degree. He and his wife employed three servants who would leave in the evening, giving the couple the time to descend into their locked

---

[28] For information on the Do X, see "World's Largest Plane Flies with Record Load," *New York Times,* 10 November 1929; "The Size of the Huge Dornier Do-X," *Science News Letter,* 15 November 1930, 307. For the flight to Berlin, see "'DoX' nach Berlin unterwegs," *Berliner Tageblatt,* 24 May 1924 (evening).

[29] "Eifersuchts-Tragödie in Berlin W.: Reisender auf offener Strasse erschossen," *Berliner Tageblatt,* 8 January 1932 (evening), and "Die Bluttat in der Motzstrasse," *Berliner Tageblatt,* 9 January 1932 (evening).

basement workshop to mint coins on their own press.[30] In its focus on public markets, the importance of money, and indeed, even in its use of a turn-screw press as a means to save the family, *What Will Become of the Children?* echoes elements of this story.

Nazism and the "Jewish Question"

Among a number of events that spoke to Germany's (and Berlin's) condition of almost covert civil war was the stabbing to death of Herbert Norkus, a member of the Hitler Youth, by Communists while he was putting up flyers advertising a meeting. In and of itself not unusual — this was an era of extreme political violence — the murder took on almost mythological dimensions when Josef Goebbels saw the propaganda value of casting Norkus as a Nazi martyr.[31] Norkus later came to be memorialized in the novel and film *Hitlerjunge Quex.* Norkus's murder in the novel resonates with the death of Helmut in chapter 6 in *What Will Become of the Children?,* although, as we will see, for Bergmann this death is merely tragic and senseless, not an unusual perspective for a Berliner to hold in 1932. As the case unfolded in the newspapers, it became known that the Communist who killed Norkus was led to him and paid by disaffected former Nazi Stormtroopers.[32] His payment for the murder: ten liters of beer; his prison sentence: six years.[33]

Perhaps most ominous in the catalogue of events that was Berlin in 1932 was the May 12 beating of Helmut Klotz. Klotz was a writer, editor, and former member of the Nazi Party until he was expelled in 1924 who later came to work with democratic organizations. He had recently published several letters exposing the homosexuality of Ernst Röhm, the violent and blustering leader of the Nazi Stormtroopers.[34] Klotz had been eating

---

[30] "Rechtsgelehrter als Falschmünzer," *Berliner Tageblatt,* 16 January 1932 (morning); Der mysteriöse Dr. Salaban," *Berliner Tageblatt,* 16 January 1932 (evening), "Das Doppelleben des Falschmünzers Salaban," *Berliner Tageblatt,* 16 January 1932 (evening), and "30000 Zweimarkstücke von Dr. Salaban angefertigt und im Umlauf gebracht," *Berliner Tageblatt,* 17 January 1932 (morning).

[31] For the story of Herbert Norkus and his enshrinement in the Nazi pantheon, see, Jay Baird, *To Die For Germany: Heroes in the Nazi Pantheon* (Indiana UP, Bloomington), 1990.

[32] a.n., "Mordgemeinschaft der Radikalen: Ehemalige S.A.-Leute stifteten Kommunisten zu der Bluttat an Norkus an," *Vossische Zeitung,* 27 February 1932 (morning).

[33] "Schwere Zuchthausstrafen im Prozess Norkus beantragt," *Berliner Tageblatt,* 14 July 1932 (evening).

[34] Ironically, it was precisely Röhm's homosexuality that Hitler highlighted when he explained to the German public why he had him executed in June 1934.

lunch with several Social Democratic Reichstag deputies in the restaurant of the Reichstag building. The deputies left the table to return to parliamentary business, leaving Dr. Klotz to finish his lunch. At this point four members of the Nazi parliamentary delegation — including Gregor Strasser, at the time a high-ranking member of the party — walked by the table, saw Klotz, one of them exclaiming, "Ach, that's the dog who forged the Röhm letters," whereupon they proceeded to beat up Klotz.[35] When the police arrived in the chamber, numbering twenty-five to thirty, and tried to take the four into custody, the scene became even more chaotic, until one of the fraction's members, Frick, told the deputy chief of police that the perpetrators would go quietly. With a final "Heil Hitler," they were led out of the chamber.[36] Ultimately three of them were sentenced to three months in jail. Strasser could not be conclusively identified, and was released.[37]

In view of the persecution of Jews later instituted by the Nazis as official policy, culminating in the horrors of the Holocaust, any discussion of the Nazis during the Weimar Republic must lead to a discussion of both anti-semitism and Jewish life in Germany at the time.[38] Several facts will certainly point to German Jewry's precarious position. The *Protocols of the Elders of Zion,* a late nineteenth century Russian forgery purporting to document a Jewish plot to control the world and perhaps the most viciously antisemitic document ever written, circulated more widely in the Weimar Republic than anywhere ever before.[39] In a real-life incident similar to one that occurs in the novel, Heinrich Buxbaum describes an antisemitic incident he experienced on a train trip:

> That evening there were seven or eight passengers sitting in the dark fourth-class compartment. They were all silent until one of them piped

[35] "Ein feiger Ueberfall. Kapitänleutnant a.D. Dr. Klotz von vier nationalsozialistischen Abgeordneten unter Führung des Fememörders Heines im Reichstag blutig geschlagen," *Berliner Tageblatt,* 12 May 1932 (evening).

[36] "Reichstag aufgeflogen. Tumultszenen bis zum Schluss. — Polizei im Plenarsaal. — Vier nationalsozialistische Abgeordnete festgenommen," *Berliner Tageblatt,* 13 May 1932 (morning).

[37] "Das Urteil des Schnellgerichts: Drei Abgeordnete zu drei Monaten Gefängnis verurteilt — Strasser freigesprochen," *Vossische Zeitung,* 14 May 1932 (morning).

[38] This brief discussion of the history of Jews in Weimar Germany is indebted to Michael Meyer, ed., *German-Jewish History in Modern Times* (New York: Columbia UP, 1998).

[39] Avraham Barkai, "Jewish Life in Its German Mileu," in Meyer, *German-Jewish History,* 48. For a brilliant refutation, see Binjamin W. Segal, *A Lie and a Libel: The History of the Protocols of the Elders of Zion,* ed. and trans. Richard S. Levy (Lincoln and London: U of Nebraska P, 1995).

up with the customary cue: "Those damn Jews, they're the ones responsible for all our misfortune." Several other passengers immediately chimed in their agreement. . . . They went on rehashing the same nonsense again and again. With each repetition this disgusting babble became more vicious and unbearable. Finally I couldn't stand it any longer . . . Naturally I prefaced my remarks by saying: "Well, I'm a Jew, etc., etc." That was just the signal they'd been waiting for. The men pounced on me . . . [and began] to jostle and push me around. One of them who was seated between me and the door . . . suggested to the others: "C'mon, let's toss the Jew out of the train." I couldn't overlook that warning and so said nothing more. . . . One of the men, whose jawing had been even more nasty than the others, got off together with me in Friedberg. I recognized him in the dimly lit station. We were members of the same soccer club, and I'd never have dreamed that this man was such a rabid antisemite.[40]

Antisemitic violence was a common occurrence. In November, 1924 an actual pogrom took place in the Scheunenviertel, a heavily Jewish district of Berlin, in which dozens were injured and more than 200 shops vandalized.[41] In September, 1931, Berlin again saw open antisemitic violence on the fashionable Kurfürstendamm during Rosh Hashanah, the Jewish New Year.[42] Between 1923 and 1932, more than 200 cases of vandalism against synagogues and Jewish cemeteries were registered across Germany.[43]

In response to this shocking upwelling of antisemitism and anti-Jewish violence, many of Germany's Jews gradually drifted away from their path towards assimilation and sought a return to a more traditional Judaism and search for Jewish community and Jewish identity. This was expressed in a growing support for Zionism, and in a new religiosity among many young German Jews. Jewish museums sprung up in major cities. New Jewish books, including a Jewish encyclopedia and the famed Martin Buber/Franz Rosenzweig translation of the Bible appeared.[44]

This attempt to create a new, vibrant German-Jewish culture ultimately would fail. In short, as the novel itself will now make clear, Berlin and Germany were almost in a state of undeclared civil war. In 1932, this almost

---

[40] Quoted in Avraham Barkai, "Jewish Life . . .," 50.

[41] Dirk Walter, *Antisemitische Kriminalität und Gewalt: Judenfeindschaft in der Weimarer Republik* (Bonn: Dietz Verlag, 1999), 151–54.

[42] Walter, *Antisemitische Kriminalität und Gewalt*, 213–21.

[43] Walter, *Antisemitische Kriminalität und Gewalt*, 251.

[44] For the story of this renewal of Jewish Culture, see Michael Brenner, *The Renaissance of Jewish Culture in Weimar Germany* (New Haven: Yale UP, 1996).

forgotten year — almost forgotten because it was so tightly wedged between the stock-market collapse that ushered in the Great Depression and the advent of the Third Reich — the history of the city is a whirlwind of hope, collapse, and violence, of birth and death. Nevertheless, as a reading of *What Will Become of the Children?* will also show, the teleology of a doomed Weimar Republic is an oversimplification. In 1932, there was some hope that Germany's international situation might improve. The Depression certainly seemed to have bottomed out, and signs pointed to some possibility of expansion. There was at least some reason to think that a better Germany might emerge in the 1930s, one based on good will, mutual understanding, advanced technology, and optimism, although perhaps not on western-style democracy. Unfortunately, as we all know, history did not take this turn.

WHAT WILL BECOME OF THE CHILDREN?

CHAPTER ONE

THE PATERFAMILIAS IS BROUGHT ONTO THE STAGE AND BECOMES A RICH MAN WITH IDEAS

WORKER, PEACETIME MILLIONAIRE, and once again, worker. That was and is the life of Herr Deutsch.

Well, to be precise, he isn't really a worker today. Getting on in years a bit, and, like all others with neither income nor money, he has to brave the crowds and go to the welfare office to withdraw some of the heavy taxes that he paid to an earlier state. But, as one who was self-employed, he doesn't receive any unemployment support. He fights — quite understandably — with the welfare office and squabbles about politics with his children and a few other people who see the world differently than he does. Still, he spends his time writing admiring letters to the former Kaiser, living in exile in Doorn.[1]

Once, before the financial crisis took his car, he drove across the Dutch border, down the clean, brick streets, as far as the Doorn estate's gate. The gatekeeper, not surprisingly, didn't let Herr Deutsch in. Later, though, Herr Deutsch did receive a letter:

". . . For the consideration that you have shown my father, I would like to thank you in his and in my name. Crown Prince Wilhelm von Preussen." Included was an autographed, recently dated photograph of the Ex-Kaiser. Herr Deutsch lives off of this.

His offspring, brought into the world in great numbers by Herr Deutsch owing to his earlier wealth, have only one comment: Pitt Deutsch is a fool. Incomprehensible. Such a pity, too. Twenty years ago he had such a good head on his shoulders.

---

[1] Upon abdicating the German Imperial throne, Kaiser Wilhelm II (1859–1941) lived the rest of his life in exile in Doorn, the Netherlands.

The first name, Pitt, is the only thing left the family from those "founder" years.[2] One of the good things about Herr and Frau Deutsch was that they didn't put on high-class airs like a lot of people who made their fortune during the war. They remained in wealth what they had been earlier: a simple, hardworking, and somewhat too stingy Berlin family. They stayed true to the city's northern districts,[3] and had no interest in a villa in Grunewald, a French governess for the children, or gold utensils for their daily use. But, when it came to his name, Herr Deutsch wanted to be called "Pitt," not "August." We will call him what he wants. There is something ponderous about all us Germans, something we would like to be rid of. . . . Whoever here recognizes his own small weaknesses is definitely a good man, but, as a German, he takes these things too seriously. And that can be enough to slow him down.

Before we turn to the more recent history of the family Deutsch, including the children, who had their own direction, perhaps we might jump back to see how Pitt Deutsch succeeded in becoming a peacetime millionaire and then lost it all.

Before 1900, Pitt Deutsch was a toolmaker. Like all skilled workers in those days, he did the journeyman's tour of the continent. His wanderings on foot led him from Berlin across the Saint Gotthard Pass in Switzerland to Italy and back again. When he got back home, he was almost unrecognizable, for accidents had occurred. For one, the St. Bernards (both dogs and monks) found him half frozen and then cared for him for weeks; for another, later on, he half starved while he wandered about Italy. You see, even then the times weren't always so brilliant. Unrecognizable, beat up, no soles on his shoes, not a coin in his pocket, a meager, soup kitchen sandwich in his stomach, he made it back to Berlin.

Berlin gave him a festive welcome. Genuine carpets hung from the windows along Unter den Linden. Thousands of wax candles burned behind countless windows. Gilded laurel wreaths and pine garlands festooned the streets. Thousands of marks worth of fireworks lit the night sky. Cannons rolled to the Brandenburg Gate and the Freedom Castle on the Spree River. Taps were sounded in the evening. A Socialist meeting in a cellar tavern somewhere along the Markus Strasse was broken up by the police. The empress gave yellow roses to patients in the hospitals.

Pitt Deutsch's heart rose up in his chest. His once military legs swung. Thrusting his walking stick in the air and shouting "Hurrah!" he tipped his

---

[2] The term Bergmann uses here, *Gründerjahre*, founding years, was also the term used to describe the early years of the German Empire, which gives the phrase an ironic edge.

[3] Berlin North was and is a largely working-class, industrial area.

shabby hat to every bemedalled uniform that paraded by. Of course, the festival didn't celebrate him and his return, but the Kaiser's birthday, and that was nice, too. Berlin was amazed. Berlin laughed: our Kaiser, our Peace-Kaiser, hip, hip, hooray! He knows how to celebrate. Money for the people, and an understanding of how the world really works. He stays true to his motto: "Whoever wants peace should prepare for war." Hooray!

As he watched the torchlit procession and the marching diplomatic corps, the manly fencing fraternities with their colors hoisted high — black — white — red: *suum cuique*, violet — white — gold: *sana mens in corpore sano*, green — blue — red: happy, loyal and true, to the friend a hand, to the enemy a forehead — by this wonderful vision of Teutons, Hevellers, Obotriten, Brandenburgiaers, Philippers, Borussens, and others, Herr Deutsch's heart swelled so mightily that he immediately thought of two things. First, he thought of his Martha. Then he thought of what he wanted to start.

It wasn't easy to find Martha. She had been working for a Jewish family on the Oranienburger Strasse in the old days when she would join him for thick slabs of liverwurst and other military treats, which she had snuck from the house. We latecomers have heard how pure, sweet, and virginal the girls of that earlier era were, but that couldn't have been true of them all. . . . Certainly not by 1900. Martha had been fired because of a secret guest she'd been keeping in her room for several days. Out of a sense of tact, though, nothing about this was reported to Herr August Deutsch, the previous boy-friend, when he now came looking for Martha. After checking with three gentlemen former "employers," he finally found her in Grünau working at a cold buffet table. She was radiant, robust, blond and — chaste. She was not against sacrificing her small savings to get married. Her diverse "gentlemen employers" provided her dowry. Later, Martha was, by the way, always intent on giving the impression that she had been chaste until the marriage ceremony took place.

So, Herr August Deutsch married, and the young couple took a small, neat apartment in Moabit. Martha's 400 marks paid for a wonderful wedding celebration, including, of course, a veil complete with myrtle wreath. A suit was bought, a frock coat was borrowed, living room and kitchen were furnished, and there was even some money left over for tools and a dog. "Martha, I will even build us a small wagon," said Herr Deutsch.

Marrying Martha had been a smart decision. But one thing Deutsch did not know: Martha knew a lot of people, all "guests" from her former life in Grünau. The frock coat was a loan from one such guest. Martha also knew a deaf man whose workshop wasn't doing so well anymore.

This workshop was set up to wash the cloths that cleaned the machine works across the street. Before the shop existed, the factory always threw these cloths away. As long as the deaf man's wife was alive, the workshop provided the family with a living. But she died in childbirth, and the child

3

soon followed. The customers, though, had no patience with the deaf man, and he didn't really know how to wash the cloths. Martha, though, was able to give him some sage advice.

Namely, they agreed that August Deutsch would bring some of his tools and that the deaf man would bring him his old customers. Martha would wash the cleaning cloths and together with her husband visit the customers, because it was important after all to realize her husband's second idea. From that point on, they would split the proceeds of the washing business fifty-fifty.

Deutsch's second idea came from the recognition of a simple fact, and the consequences of that recognition. On the whole, it was much easier then to grab opportunities, because there were still real opportunities then, and not just artificially produced ones. In those days, skilled workers had their own tools and did not, like today, get them from the employer.

Even if they were more primitive than today's complicated machine tools, it still was a heavy blow for the worker when they gave out or were lost. Deutsch couldn't help if tools were lost, but he could fix wear and tear.

He could reforge chisels, clean out files, sharpen saws, and reface hammers. Those were the sorts of work that Deutsch decided to make his own. On certain days of the week he and his wife would take their dogcart through town and collect old files, saws, hammers, and dirty cleaning cloths, giving out claim checks for them. On other days they would distribute the same, improved, tools for a fee of a few pennies. Sometimes the tools might be a little shorter, and the cloths a little lighter. Martha also made sure that the deaf man didn't always get half of the proceeds, because she believed that she and her husband did more than half of the work. But on the whole, Herr Deutsch saw to it that things were run honorably.

The dogcart business flourished. Soon they had to employ in addition to the deaf man a second, third, and even a fourth hand to help out. The washtubs grew too small for the cloths; the nights before delivery days, August Deutsch worked renewing the tools. Soon, they had to rent a cellar to keep the tools in; even large businesses with their own equipment began to use the Deutsch family. Nobody suspected that this penny business could make somebody rich.

Despite their monopoly, and their growing business, Deutsch, with his wife and their dogcart, showed up punctually at the factory gates. "Punctuality is half of life, Martha," Pitt said to his wife. They picked up and then returned tools again as quickly as possible. Perhaps because of this modesty nobody realized what an upturn their business had taken.

When good fortune first extends its hand, it often remains loyal. Their deaf partner died after three years of zealous activity. He had no heirs and, so, with a thankful smile for the Deutschs, the deaf man left them almost his entire share for the three years in gratitude for the care Frau Deutsch had shown him.

With her first child on the way, Frau Deutsch decided it was time to leave the dogcart behind. After the burial, Deutsch took his wife to the Egg House, a café in Treptow, where one of his friends from the old days, Maxie Graf — the military musician — was playing. Deutsch knew him from their long-ago days in the army and introduced himself. The party developed into a great drinking fest, with the result that the men had to hang on to the Litfass poles that abound in Berlin.[4] It occurred to Martha, for the first time in a long while, as she eyed the good-looking military musician, 2nd Guard Regiment, Infantry, that she was still a pretty classy woman. From the Egg House they moved on to Eggebrecht, where the upstanding middle-class world drank their wine. Feeling ever so sophisticated, Frau Deutsch vowed to take her husband out much more frequently.

On the other hand, August Deutsch woke up the next morning, looked at his wallet, and thought that he had not had such a blowout in six years, and that he could do quite well for six years more without another. And since the acquisition of money per se required the suppression of personal wishes, he looked forward with equanimity to more years of serious, hard work. The only exception to that was to be the Kaiser's birthday: then he and his wife, wearing their best clothes, would join the parade down the illuminated street, Unter den Linden. After a few years their children, in their blue sailor suits, would join the fun.

Thus the rise of Pitt Deutsch happened relatively quickly.

He didn't allow himself leisurely walks or meetings in the pubs with friends. His wife never had more than 100 marks a month to run the household. He would clop his children if they ruined something, even if they got so much as a stain on their Sunday clothes. If they brought home good grades, they earned a new piece of clothing; if their grades were poor, they earned a spanking. One day, though, Frau Deutsch stated flatly, "I'm finished laundering oily cleaning cloths." Herr Deutsch rejoined that she wouldn't need a maid anymore, either. Their apartments grew a bit over time, but never grew bigger than three rooms in the district of Moabit. One, of course, was the 'good room', only for Sundays and visitors.

Visitors, though, were few and far between. Herr Deutsch didn't like visitors very much because they ate too much of what somebody else had

---

[4] Litfass poles (Litfaßsäulen) are a Berlin institution. They are large cement cylinders, distributed about the city, on which notices for upcoming cultural, club, and political events are posted. They would be especially conspicuous in the Weimar Republic because of all of the election posters mounted on them.

worked hard to buy. He fought with Martha about this on several occasions. She wanted so badly to show her family and friends their new salon with its real silverware and artificial palm tree, the now-fulfilled realization of the dream of all her years as a household servant. But Herr Deutsch didn't even speak with her for eight days, eight days in which he worked even harder on his new discovery, eight days in which the argument was only Martha's. Finally an argument broke out on its own.

For a time, his new discovery drove Pitt Deutsch up a wall. But Pitt was not a man who would sit around and do nothing, well — not yet. He was always adjusting his machinery, upgrading this and that; he read technical books to the extent that his limited technical education would allow; he was always tinkering, always thinking. Over time he developed a mechanical cloth washer. This gave him the idea that bakeries could use something similar to knead their dough. He didn't have the facilities to build this himself, but he sold the model to a cookie factory for a very good price. He used the money for ever-newer pursuits, especially his newest idea of replacing hand tools with mechanized ones.

His old penny trade gave him access to businesses, and they were all interested in his ideas. Soon little August Deutsch had become the great machine-tool maker Pitt Deutsch, with access to foreign markets and to imports.

The most significant luxuries that he allowed his family were a five-room apartment, higher education for the children, a piano, and a live-in maid. Martha was closely involved in planning the children's schooling. As was to be expected of a simple woman, she idolized "educated men" and wanted her children to have this aura about them. She was armed with ideas, always laying into her husband about just how and where the children should be educated. He finally gave up, even swallowing his favorite saying, "A hard-working man can become anything he wants to be, even without school: just look at me."

About a year before Princip, a completely unimportant man, lit the fuse for the Great War, Pitt Deutsch's workshop and newest machines had put a cool million into his bank account.[5]

But he was not the kind of man who could sit around and enjoy his leisure. During the Tangier Crisis, which he didn't quite understand (Herr Deutsch was like most Germans of his time: his political education was one-

---

[5] Gavrilo Princip assassinated the Archduke Franz Ferdinand, heir to the Austrian throne, on June 28, 1914, setting off a series of diplomatic maneuverings and crises resulting in the outbreak of the First World War.

sided and full of German sentimentality) and during the war scares of 1909 and 1911 Pitt Deutsch began to think about one of the practical consequences of a war. One of his strongest characteristics was to be able to achieve great things from small ideas. Here, too, he had much in common with his countrymen.

After all, if something wasn't invented in Germany, where was it perfected? In Germany. He didn't always have brilliant insight, but he could be counted on for extraordinarily patient, thorough, hard work and critical reflection.

But when Pitt Deutsch fell upon the particulars of a big problem and started to concentrate on a point that at first seemed to be a very isolated, secondary issue, this is what happened: Pitt had a headache and didn't want to see anyone from his family. He couldn't work. He had no friends; at most he spoke one time with a few other manufacturers about issues that didn't have anything to do with the problem at hand. So what did Pitt do? He went to the movies to relax. Even in those days films didn't really tax their audiences.

Pitt goes to a film in which Arabs attack a French fort, destroy the telegraph station, and sabotage the wells.[6] The soldiers in the fort defend themselves as well as they can, but their weapons are not yet as varied as in later times, when people claimed to want an end to wars. The soldiers can't gas the Arabs, they can't build an electric perimeter around the fort, they can't take pills to substitute for water. In short, they lose everything. Water, their lives, their munitions. With a wild "Ay! Ay!" — seemingly the cry of the desert — the Arabs conquer the dead French. "Damn. Another crummy film," Herr Deutsch complains to himself.

Pitt, though, keeps playing it over in his mind: "OK, let's imagine that we, Germany, were being attacked from all sides. Now, I know that's not likely. We're related to the English. Ditto with the Russians, and we're friends, too. We're allied with Austria. Switzerland and Holland are neutral. Our only real enemies are the French, our arch foes. Still, let's imagine that we're encircled like the fort. If we were too efficient for the English . . . and those anarchists in Russia really can't be trusted. And the Austrians, . . . Alright, anyway, let's say that it happened. What would we be really short of? Water? No. It would take too much poison to ruin our water supply. Wheat, sure, we could run out of it, but unless the war is in the middle of the country we can grow enough grain and potatoes." Pitt runs through the possibilities, one after another. He sees some things in very short supply, but there's enough to last out an emergency. He sticks with the assumption that

---

[6] At this point in the narrative, the text changes from past tense to present tense, which it will generally — with some exceptions — maintain until the end.

the Arabs haven't yet gotten into the fort. He trusts Krupp for cannons and for guns. They have stockpiles of resources, not like him, who is constantly having to order raw materials in small quantities. Abruptly he stops and thinks, "What about chemicals? In medicine they can often be replaced with herbs or surrogates; paper can replace wadding. But there's no way you can shoot with herbs. He laughed a light-hearted laugh and came to the conclusion that each of the munitions factories in the world have enough supplies to blow up half of the world's capital cities. He continued to turn the problem over in his head on the way home, all the more so because he was poorly informed about whether there was anything that cannons needed to fire that might run out. The thought wouldn't stop bedeviling him, and at first he couldn't find anybody whom he could ask.

Then, one day, a happy accident occurred. A customer in Essen bought one of his especially complicated machine tools.[7] This, in turn, necessitated several technical discussions. Such meetings might give one some interesting insights into manufacturing needs, even despite the security precautions. Pitt Deutsch learned no state secrets, but he did find out by and by that to fire, cannons needed sealing rings, a fact known to every student at a technical university. Soon he also knew that the rings needed shellac. This, in turn, led him to the fact that shellac was an import. One of shellac's properties was its ability to swell and shrink according to the season. Shellac couldn't be stored in large quantities. Its trade was not in governmental hands. Compared with its uses, stockpiles were small. There were, however, very few firms that didn't use the yellow and brown scales or amber-like clumps of shellac that could only be acquired by tapping fig trees. Shellac would disappear faster than rubber or leather if the borders were blockaded. Even a non-chemist like Pitt Deutsch quickly grasped that shellac was almost irreplaceable.

It wasn't enough to fabricate a synthetic resin. That already existed. Rather, a substance was needed that had all of shellac's properties but wouldn't break down. To be able to create this would be useful even if no war came. Perhaps it would serve to lower shellac's price.

Martha could no longer join Pitt's restless, striving flight forward. Accordingly, he hardly spoke to her anymore. He built a laboratory and engaged the services of a chemist largely ruined by too much schnapps and heroin. The latter called "Herr Pitt" his "Friend and Dear Chap" and went on and on — especially when he was drunk — about how much he knew about different chemical processes.

Pitt Deutsch started a program of tutelage and self-study and, after an entire additional year, earned the results that he was working for. Finally he

[7] Although the text does not state this explicitly, all Germans at the time would have known that Essen was the home of Krupp, Germany's largest weapons manufacturer.

had his LACAID, a most useful isolation material that could stretch shellac. The academically trained drunken chemist was impertinent, wasted a lot of cash, brewed his own schnapps instead of conducting experiments, and claimed that LACAID was his invention and his alone. We, naturally, know better. Pitt Deutsch, not the chemist, was the father of LACAID. All that our Pitt learned from his employee were the basic principles of chemistry, the principles that tired professors crammed into this wastrel's head between fencing bouts and long nights in bars. And, indeed, for this Pitt paid a considerable sum and didn't pay particularly close attention to the hours that the man worked. You would think he would be grateful to Herr Deutsch, since no one else had been willing to employ such a waste of a human being. Instead, he hit him with a lawsuit.

This, naturally, happened after Pitt Deutsch had dismissed the chemist. He never disputed the chemist's part in the invention. Herr August Deutsch was ordered to pay 20 percent of the value of this discovery to the plaintiff.

Perhaps we can now say that with this judgment Fate was warning Herr Deutsch, "My dear Pitt, be careful. Your luck is running out." Pitt, however, was not interested in such omens. He simply said that, "Whoever rolls in the mud is sure to get dirty. I'll never hire such a scoundrel again."

CHAPTER TWO

WAR BREAKS OUT IN A PARK, AND HERR DEUTSCH COMES TO THE AID OF HIS FATHERLAND

A ND YET, FATE'S WARNING did not seem to be so loud. LACAID enjoyed immediate success. One day Pitt Deutsch decided that he really ought to do something with his family, and decided to take them to an afternoon concert in the Pankow Park.

He really loved the suburb of Pankow, nestled between two parks. Indeed, he planned to buy a villa here, on the quiet Park Strasse, or perhaps a bit farther out in Niederschoenhausen near the old Schlosspark. He hadn't told his family about this, not yet. In fact, it brought to mind the 20,000 marks that the court had had him pay that scoundrel. If it hadn't been for him, Pitt could have fulfilled his wishes without even touching his capital. He knew for a fact that the Bleichroeder villa was available for just a little more.[1] Not too big, with a beautiful garden. Just the kind of place where a man could relax. Of course, he would also keep his city home; he wasn't ready to retire just yet.

Frau Martha was pleased with his wonderfully calm mood. The children had cake with real cream, and then looked around the park and onto the tennis courts that still smelled like stables. Klara and Elsa were two very pretty young things. Although Elsa was still a child, something about her made her seem older. As the music played, they strolled along the promenade in their slit skirts like two proper young ladies, catching the eyes of the young men lounging about. Their family's bank account also got them some attention, . . . and some giggles, too. Klara swung her parasol — even though the sun had already set — and Elsa picked at the cherry-festooned velvet ribbon hanging from her hat as if she wanted to pluck them out.

A fraternity member, dappled Great Dane at his side, threw his handkerchief onto the sidewalk, picked it up again, hurried over to the girls, and asked if one of the young ladies had lost her kerchief. This new acquaintanceship got off on the right foot, and tossing his walking stick into the

---

[1] Gerson von Bleichroeder was a well-known nineteenth-century German-Jewish banker.

air, he never left their side. The threesome wandered off from the promenade toward the romantic Panke River. Colorful clothes, caps, and uniforms abounded.

On this beautiful, sunny summer day two young, gray-clad girls shyly looked about as they waded through the little stream. Within minutes, a policeman and a nun appeared under the hanging willows of the clear, rippling Panke's other bank. They called out, "Have you seen two girls? They've run away!" Elsa quickly responded, "No!"

"Why did you say 'no'? We did see them. They have tightly knotted hair." With this she touched her own Schiller-like locks.

"If they ran away, it's because they couldn't take it anymore! Let them go. I just hope they get away."

"Where could they be from? They looked like orphans."

Here the student chimed in. "They're certainly from over there, at Siloah."

When Klara asked what Siloah was, he answered, "Nothing for your ears, my dear Miss."

"Then it is surely an institute for the moral improvement of girls who've fallen into sin," rebutted Elsa.

Reddening with anger, Klara retorted, "Elsa, I'm shocked!"

With a light smile, the student "poured oil onto troubled waters": "Now, now. It's not just fallen girls, there are some there, too, whose grandmother has kicked them out."

Elsa knitted her brows together and thought out loud. "A girl just left our school when people saw that she was expecting. She didn't go to Siloah, though. She went into the country, and we heard that she's happily married."

"Elsa, I don't understand you." Klara jumped up from the bank and walked along the path. The student jumped up, too, took Elsa with one arm, his dog with the other, and tried to mend fences with Klara.

"My dear Miss, Miss Klara. There's nothing wrong with your sister; she's just a modern girl. Just a little untamed. These days they talk about anything. I don't see anything the matter with it. Why are you so angry? You two are a lovely pair. And, if I may say so, you are very pretty when you're angry. Now, please, be good again and do give me another smile."

Elsa would have been very happy to call her older sister a "silly goose" — because Klara's prudishness embarrassed her, not because of her own tomboyish remarks. For the sake of peace, though, she decided to keep her mouth shut.

They started back down the Lasterallee, which, all of a sudden, seemed yet busier than before. Even the student thought that the people looked like a flock of chickens with their heads cut off.

"You mean there are more people than usual?"

"No, but they look so confused." He looks up to his left, where his fraternity brothers are sitting, or, at the moment, standing, with serious faces. In fact they're more screaming than singing "Deutschland, Deutschland über alles" with the most peculiarly empty faces. They quickly move on to another song, "We will always be true to you."

The student yells up to one of his friends, Horst, to ask what they're celebrating on this hellishly hot afternoon.

"Where have you been hiding yourself? Read the telegram."

"What telegram?"

"Move along, move along please. We want to see it too." With this a small group, including a tall, thin, haggard, deadly-serious man, pushes past the two girls and their new friend. As the man passes, they hear a snatch of what he is saying: "Murder, that means war!"

Finally they make their way to a restaurant, "The Upper House," full of sweating waiters struggling with coffee cups and beer mugs. The news must have even made its way up to the bandstand, stopping the players in the middle of their schmaltzy sea chantey.

A deathlike calm falls over the park, leaving only the dust dancing in the air to remind people that the sun still shone. Abruptly, the music restarts, "Deutschland, Deutschland über Alles" joined by a chorus, thousands strong.

At the same time our three young people read a note pinned to the restaurant's kitchen door:

MURDER IN SARAJEVO!

When the crowd soon started jostling again, Klara asked who was murdered. "Was it our Kaiser or his wife? Was it a prince?"

"As far as I could tell it was an Austrian archduke. I think his wife, too. But I wasn't able to read it all."

"My God, that has nothing to do with us!" says Klara, and Elsa, with her strong grasp of geography, throws in her two cents:

"In any case Sarajevo isn't even in Germany. And was the murderer even a German? It sounds like a Balkan matter. So why are dark rumors of war being brought up everywhere? Is it our fault if something happens in some other country? I'd like to ask Father what he thinks it means."

Still smiling, they promised to meet the student in Wolf Wertheim's incredibly modern arcade department store for a stroll at 6:00. With this, they headed to their parents' house for dinner.

While Pitt Deutsch was looking for his "rascals," the two minnows, he stumbled upon the telegram. The headline, MURDER IN SARAJEVO, froze him to the marrow. He never was able to explain why, and the other thing he never could explain was why his inner eye saw the word LACAID floating in type

13

just as large. Although he wasn't going to worry about international alliances and other such things, he also lacked the girls' healthy logic: that other countries' affairs simply weren't Germany's concern, and that nobody could hold Germans responsible for them. Rather, Pitt Deutsch had only one thought: the very next morning he was going to march down to the Ministry of War and tell them about LACAID. It wasn't that he had any expectations of or vision of what might follow from this murder. His political naiveté was only matched by his lack of interest; he relied fully on his Peace Kaiser. He didn't even know the names of most of the Ministers on the Wilhelmstrasse.[2] Certainly he knew of Bismarck, Eulenburg, Hohenlohe, and Bülow — he'd read about them in the *Berliner Lokalanzeiger*, which told him all that a good German ought to know.[3] But on the other hand, even the secret power of Holstein was unknown to him.[4]

Now and again his wife would suggest that they cancel the *Lokalanzeiger* and replace it with the *Berliner Morgenpost*, which had a better entertainment section, but Pitt didn't think he would learn anything new or different from a different newspaper. After all, didn't they all share the same censor?

Pitt Deutsch didn't think about any of this. He was only concerned with one thing: every invention had to be brought to the attention of his Fatherland, especially those that were important for the war effort. Otherwise, one was no better than a traitor. So, without further ado, he prepared to go to the Ministry of War the very next day.

When he arrived, Pitt Deutsch found everybody so busy that it was hard to get anyone's attention. Men ran back and forth so much as to create a vision of a flock of headless chickens. Oddly, though, Pitt also thought that they seemed to be very unapproachable.

"War? My dear Herr Deutsch — that is your name, isn't it — why would anybody think about war? With our Kaiser? And even if there were a war" — here he smiled his superior smile — "we wouldn't need half of the stock of shellac that we already have. We are so well armed that I can say the following, with absolute confidence: because of the technical materiel that we

[2] The Wilhelmstrasse was the traditional center of Imperial Germany's governmental power, much like Pennsylvania Avenue in Washington, DC or Downing Street in London.

[3] These four were all nineteenth-century governmental ministers. All but Eulenburg served as imperial chancellor.

[4] Friedrich von Holstein (1837–1909), although never foreign minister, was an important voice in the formation of imperial German foreign policy. Some liberals believed that some of his ideas and positions had helped move Germany towards war.

and our enemies have, no war could last more than two months, a quarter year at the longest. There is no question that our stockpiles will suffice. But, if you would leave your sample and the formula, I will nevertheless direct it to the right department. I promise that they will be in touch." —

"Mother, dear, don't cry your eyes out. We'll be home in a quarter year at the longest." Such was the common phrase, a few weeks later, of the boys in field gray, marching to war because of a promise made to the Austrians.

Relatively quickly, after only three months to be exact, Pitt Deutsch received a refusal from the Ministry of War: there was no need for his product. At the same time, because of the war, of course, he was prohibited from marketing his product to any other customers.

This certainly made Pitt Deutsch grumpy, and when Peter, his oldest son, asked him if he should volunteer for the army, Pitt slapped him in the face.

"Isn't it enough that your father's been called into the Landsturm, you stupid boy?"

For some reason, Pitt Deutsch wasn't terrifically enthusiastic about the war. Perhaps if the Ministry of War had wanted LACAID he might have felt differently. One can never know.

On the whole we can say that at first Pitt and his family were barely touched by the war. As none of the family was in the field, they didn't spend their days and nights worrying. Worrying when the postman arrived with his good or bad news wasn't part of their routine. Herr Deutsch had had the reassuring feeling of being a good German from the start, having turned far more than half of his liquid assets into war bonds. Frau Deutsch, now a wealthy woman, didn't much trouble herself so much about ration coupons for bread, flour, potatoes, butter, shoes, and clothing rations that were soon to come. For one thing there was always an "element" who would sell these things at a reasonable price. Secondly they could drive their car, purchased just before the war's outbreak, into the countryside, where farmers could always be found who would gladly sell produce to customers willing to pay better prices. Unlike millions of other women, the wives of soldiers, workers, and government officials, Martha, the former serving girl, didn't need to spend her nights trying to prepare meals from meager groceries and her days replacing men in offices, the postal service, street cars or railways. Her time wouldn't be spent turning rifle barrels in arms factories. The fortunate Martha had to worry neither about her beloved husband nor about bread for her children.

Indeed, for the Family Deutsch, the war provided a nice break from the daily routine. As people used to say in those days, their war was inside, because outside the weather was bad. The extra editions of the newspapers, the train stations full of men in field gray — this was all so terribly interesting.

Even though it was more difficult than in the prewar days to get materials to make the machine tools, the business flourished to a certain extent because the growing needs of military producers brought advantages to Herr Deutsch both in acquiring resources and in his workers' having draft exemptions. From now on, women would do all of the less technical work, and they also had the advantage of being cheaper to employ than men.

Another nice little benefit for Herr Deutsch was that as an indirect producer of military materials, he had the right to reduce his workers' wages almost by half, even though his income stayed the same as before the war. Frau Martha followed in his footsteps, in that although she was still getting supplied well and sufficiently with foodstuffs and the like, she only gave her serving girl what her card entitled her to.

We needn't think too much about all of this; isn't it often the case that the self-made "little man" becomes the stingiest employer?

All of a sudden it was the end of 1915 — five quarter years had come and gone — and everywhere one looked the initial enthusiasm for the war seemed to have given way to deep reservations, even in families who hadn't lost a son or a father. Of course people still believed the news reports of German armies piling victory upon victory. For one thing, foreign newspapers didn't find their way into the country. If they had, even patriotic Germans might have wondered how the enemy could also claim strings of victories. Battlefield letters home complained, asking "When will we see the homeland again?" Women were nearing the end of their ropes, and one had to really wonder how much longer could they bear this before they lost their minds. But their resilience must have been just as well developed as that of their men. On the city's outskirts the homeless slept without even a blanket, on beds of raw, uncovered straw, living hand to mouth. The first malnourished children came into the world, crying in vain at their mothers' dry breasts.

Because there was no butter, the rotting potatoes were stewed into a barley-coffee brew. Officers were forbidden from showing themselves to the enemy, as so many of the old families had already been decimated. In the city's center, and in a few of the western streets, pretentious black marketers and reserve officers made themselves at home, visiting race tracks, running up debts, drinking streams of champagne, and buying dress uniforms. They had frivolous conversations about the war and didn't even want to hear about muster camps, but still considered themselves to be born officers. If there was no bread, they were happy to eat oysters. They talked of the death they faced; should they have to wait for a girl? Not a chance. "My dear, tomorrow I could be shot through the chest. Give me the best that you have, in case I, you know. Ach, it would be lovely. If you won't, another will. Please be so good. I have no time!"

The relationship between the sexes took a radical turn.

Provincials who came to Berlin at this time only saw a few areas and said: "And Berlin is still dancing!" In every city on the front, this kind of excess was sanctioned. Soldiers needed to blow off steam before death. But nobody saw the dance palaces — or the bordellos — of Brussels, Metz, and Warsaw as the cities' true face. Even though Berlin's wilder district was only four or five streets and some racetracks, a small area for the walking dead to celebrate one last time, these streets came to symbolize the city as a whole.

At first Pitt Deutsch was happy to have his middle-class home filled with officers. The two rascals loved it, and besides, the food and the wine were good. Their parents even allowed a little dancing to the gramophone behind closed doors. But then Pitt Deutsch saw that he would have to keep a sharp eye on Klara and Elsa. Frau Deutsch, though, was ready to indulge the new manners. To her the young men seemed so nice and polite. "Certainly our girls will marry soon." Two daughters almost ready to marry and now Martha realized that she and Pitt would have a little surprise of their own soon.

In short, only Pitt Deutsch paid any attention to the comings and goings. Was he right, being so strict with his two almost-grown daughters? One can never know. Perhaps, if they had married two of the young men who were swirling about, they might have found a kind of primitive happiness. Then again, they might have lost the opportunity to develop themselves.

Then, out of nowhere, a bomb comes crashing into Pitt Deutsch's life. A letter from the Ministry of War arrives sometime during early 1916. Pitt is young again. Both he and his LACAID are needed. First he hurries to a wrong address, for in his excitement he has missed the fact that his department is in the newly expanded Hedemann Strasse.

Negotiations back and forth. Shellac stores continue to dwindle. The war manufacturers divide and share it. Everywhere one turns, people are thinking about the red-gold leaves and the gold-yellow balls — shellac in its beautiful raw form — Unter den Linden, Mauer Strasse, the lengthened Hedemann Strasse, in Saxony, indeed, even in Warsaw. Rubber goods are a serious consideration. Gamboge, a poison, also plays a role.[5] An important governmental office with directors and thousands of bureaucrats as well as middle managers, hundreds of different formulations are all in play. Rudimentary laboratories are at work deriving soaps and margarines from materials that have never produced soaps and margarines before. Binder is the word of the day. Binders are needed to hold these misbegotten materials together. Housewives open the margarine and are astonished to find cloudy

---

[5] This obscure sentence is difficult to decipher. Gamboge looks very much like shellac, and might have been substituted for it by unscrupulous war profiteers.

spots in it and that it tastes strangely like soap. The soap itself becomes gray and sandy like the soldiers.

Herr Pitt Deutsch simply shakes his head. Finally he will be reimbursed for the money that he had to pay that worthless student. Finally. The negotiations take a quarter year. There never appears to be any hurry. At last he receives a contract to produce large quantities of LACAID, but he has to change the formula. He can't use so much shellac, as there is very little left. Pitt Deutsch is astounded by the shortsightedness of it all. "I warned them a long time ago."

But then he went in joyfully and signed over the rest of his fortune to be invested in war bonds.

The LACAID business went well. Because of his importance Pitt was released from the secondary reserves. What would become of the nation if a man like Pitt Deutsch were forced into shovel service? Now, though, as a direct manufacturer for the war effort, he had to pay full wages. Nothing is perfect.

Still, he makes enough money to fulfill his dream. The villa is long since sold, but there is another nearby, ever larger and more beautiful than the last, and, according to Martha, "More Modern!" The children are rather embarrassed. Knowing that they are already wealthy, they think that people will take them for moneygrubbers.

Still there is a lesson to be learned, namely that in the old days people first earned money and only then lived a life of luxury.

Once again fate had decided to be kind, and as far as Herr Deutsch was concerned, the war could continue for a while. Max, only half grown, states with great assurance that, "Father will surely have a monument and the newspapers could very easily write about his great invention. If they don't, it's only because he won't bang his own drum loudly enough."

"I wish I had your problems," responded Peter, who was a very mature thinker for his years. "It would be better if this dreadful war would end, but Father is one of the people who are keeping it going. We'd be better off if we could just stop it right now."

"I see. So you'd rather just give in and then pay up?" Max's temperature started to rise.

"Brother, you're too young to understand: either way we're going to pay. You probably think that everything will be great again just as soon as the war's over, too?"

"God! You sound like an old man. Just let Father hear your nonsense. Just like we've held out so long against so many enemies, we'll continue to hold out, and someday they will see just how tough a people we are. Then we'll have peace — and the others will have to pay for it."

"It's possible that everybody will get tired of the war, but whether the others pay is a totally different question. What's going to happen, though, if America gets really involved?"

"Why should they? It's Europe's war, not America's problem."

Peter shrugged his shoulders at this: "The murder in Sarajevo wasn't our problem, either."

"Come off of it. The murder in Sarajevo? Europe was ready to explode. My teacher says that wars are a necessary consequence of overpopulation."

"So that's all he has to say about the dead bodies of his comrades spread all over Europe? Nice cultural theory for a pedagogue. In other words, you think that a culturally advanced people with a great civilization can't find any solution for its growing population other than war, war that destroys its own culture? If you and your teacher believe this, then the giants of German culture lived for nothing, and you're doomed to destruction."

"Peter, you know it's so complicated and maybe I'm too young to understand it all. Still, I have to believe and listen to the others. But I've recently thought what you just said, even though I couldn't have said it as well as you can. Now don't laugh, but I looked for a reason why they spilled so much blood for a bald hill I read about. We took it, but the losses were so high. Four hundred men died on it. Four hundred men are more important than a bald hill, aren't they, Peter?"

"Good job, Max! Your teacher would probably say that if the hill can grow enough food for four hundred people, then the hill is as valuable as the men who died on it. And if there weren't any more fertile territory in the whole wide world, he might even be right."

Now Max was really confused. "But, then, who's right?"

"As long as every country guards its borders and doesn't let anybody in, he's probably right. It has to do with all of humanity, get it? With good will and with unity. Then we could all sit down and divide what's out there. That would be good for people and for countries, too. What would America be today if so many energetic people hadn't emigrated there? It would just be a big, empty wasteland. There's lots of fertile land, enough for everybody to grow their own bread. But people and races are so obsessed with each other and with their own territory that they don't care about anyone else. Each group thinks that it's better than the other, and then is afraid of mixing, even though this usually refreshes a race. And besides, we're all human beings. Do you understand Max, *human beings,* who in their efforts at furthering their own civilizations, are just trying to keep up with each other, and, when there's no war, exchange their ideas, music, and so on? But war builds walls between them still higher, and then they just start to hate each other."

"Peter, that's awful. Now I'm just confused!"

Peter kept after the boy mercilessly. "Basically, a people doesn't send soldiers to die for the sake of the nation. Instead innocent people are sent out to fight and die for the sake of certain individuals and their lust for power. If only people weren't ordered into the war, but instead everyone was allowed to vote on whether they would lay down their own lives!"

"But Peter, they were all so enthusiastic to march off to war. At least that's how it looked. And the Germans, at least, look like they're happy to be soldiers."

"I can't say anything about that, Max. I'm not much older than you are. But, first of all, I doubt if *everyone* was so glad to be drafted. I'm sure their parents felt differently. Secondly, you can't forget that the long peace that we had made us a rather sleepy people. Enthusiasm and running with the crowd are infectious. Don't forget that! Germans forgot that wars have consequences. I wish that everybody, not just the Germans, could have seen the consequences before they started and then made their decisions. But you'll see: just like we're not able to enjoy a proper, happy youth now, our adulthood will be shadowed by this war too. But people will forget the consequences pretty quickly, and let themselves be driven by new powers into yet another fight."

That's how one wise young man spoke with his brother, often deep into the night — at least until their mother would march into their room and order them to be quiet and to go to sleep.

Thus began the age of brooding youth. In retrospect there is no question that Peter was a deeper thinker, more logical and more concerned with doing the right thing than, for example, his brother Jürgen, who was seven years younger. Jürgen, his friends, and their baby brother Helmut, yet again seven years younger, were more likely to be supporters of others' ideas than thinkers themselves.

Very soon after this conversation, America became an active belligerent in this war, raising the ante from merely sending supplies to the Western allies. Now when Europe's breath rattled, America gave it an injection. Only the Quakers helped the Germans, and then only when the American government let them. What did the Germans do to offend God? Poor Germany, beaten upon from all sides. And the people? The people were frugal and modest. Certainly they had never done anything to hurt anybody. Yet they suffered for all: shabby, worn out, moldy shoes on their feet; turnips and sawdust-meal bread in their stomachs; clothing that barely deserved the name on their backs, and nothing left in their closets. Every family had its own dead to mourn. Every forty-two seconds another German soldier fell on the field of honor. Mortality rates climbed behind the lines, too. For the first time in Germany, influenza reared its head, most horribly among undernourished women and children. Yet, they were still hard working, so hard working. This alone annoyed Germany's enemies. But it was never enough. America sent fresh, well-rested, and wonderfully healthy young men into the field as an offering to the West. The Germans were too tired to fight on.

Then, strange things began to happen. For one thing, friendly young men came from overseas, enthusiastic to shake hands. They were so full of life with their leather shoes and pristine uniforms, their backpacks full of food; even their basic understanding of human nature seemed so sound. Yet that didn't stop them from acting like the hounds of hell.

Then everything fell apart. For finally Siegfried the warrior was vulnerable. Germany's brave hero had held out long enough. No one will easily match his bravery. Then, again, everything changed. The malnourished German seemed to disappear as quickly as he had arrived. But his emaciated body was not yet down for good. It rose up once again. Shots were fired in Kiel and a bloody wall rose across the Frankfurter Allee in Berlin. A few shots were fired in other places as well, but we needn't think about those. Once again the quiet, contemplative Germans proved their superiority to the Russians, at least when it came to calm. Trucks armed with machine guns, called back from the front, drove though the cities; a few epaulettes and medals were torn off and thrown into the streets: in world historical terms, a rather harmless revolution. Nevertheless, we know that this was an important slice of time. It was now that the Germans began to tear at their own flesh.

CHAPTER THREE

_____

THE FAMILY GATHERS ITS EXPERIENCES, AND PITT DOES NOT UNDERSTAND HOW TO STEER HIS SHIP THROUGH THE INFLATION

PITT DEUTSCH REVERED HIS KAISER as much as ever. Could it be that he was not getting much information on the Kaiser's doings? As always, he was either poorly informed or totally uninformed about contemporary politics. Even when some things didn't add up in his head, his reverent heart could always find reasons to excuse the Kaiser. For one thing, the republic had not yet done much good for him.

At the very beginning of the revolution, the "Reds" shot out a couple of his factory windows. Pitt couldn't closely analyze the concept "the Reds" because he never put forth the effort to consider the thinking of others. Thus he lumped together the Social Democrats, Communists, Bolsheviks, even the Democrats, in short, every group that didn't love the good old days as much as he did. He had no idea who gave the order to shoot at his factory or who told his workers to stop their "murderous" activities. There were no fatalities.

Things didn't improve with the rest of his business, either. The market for LACAID collapsed just as he ordered new machinery to produce it. And his machine tool division, which had already seemed to be asleep for the last two years of the war, showed no interest in coming back to life.

At the same time, it's fair to say, the years hadn't been kind to his wife. Hard as it may be to believe, she had a series of hysterical episodes. Just think about how much more right to these episodes other women had, women who had been through much more and had more at stake in the war. Fair enough, she had given birth to seven children, but, then again, so had Germany's empress. But with Martha the situation was really not so pretty anymore. She cried at every opportunity, and had these strange attacks. She watched her children slowly starve.

And the three little ones are such sweet children, not in the least rude or wild. Susi is a little cuddle bug. Jürgen is, it's true, a bit absent minded. And Helmut, the little "mistake," is a bit puny. He's so small and pale; he just won't grow.

23

In the meantime, there is a rather sad story about Elsa, who does look to be a bit older than twenty. Where does that girl get her stubbornness? It's so unpleasant. They simply took her away. She had to go with them. His daughter. Even in school, her teachers always wrote on her report card, "Conduct acceptable at best. She is often forward." She just refuses to grow out of it. Pitt Deutsch had quite the shock when he was called to the Blücher Barracks to get his daughter.

The putsches and the strikes are enough to drive one insane. Wait; is there a putsch attempt now? It is so hard to keep them straight: Kapp Putsch, Ehrhardt, Organization Consul, Heimwehr, The Red First of May and all the street unrest. Nobody can feel safe anymore. Wasn't the war long enough? And nobody can quite sort it out. Who is this new character, Knüppelkunze? Is he German National, or is he Folkish? And did the prosecutor Bohmke insult the republic or did he not? Why were the Bergstrasse and the Podbielski Allee barricaded with barbed wire, but not the other streets?[1]

Why did they overturn the streetcar on May 1? Was somebody important inside it? Peter talks away nonchalantly about the General German Ring of Arms, a university dueling society, and about the police raiding university saber-dueling fraternities looking for weapons.[2] We even hear that Germans are serving with the Russian White Army. All very strange.

Pitt Deutsch can't follow it. He's like so many other parents who are confused by their childrens' serial affiliations with Knüppelkunze, Ehrhardt, Kapp, Organization C, General German Ring of Arms, Orgesch, Tannen-

---

[1] Some of these once-contemporary references have become quite obscure. The Kapp Putsch was a right-wing attempt to overthrow the young Weimar Republic in 1920. Hermann Erhardt was not only involved in the putsch attempt, but was the head of Organization Consul, the Freikorps (paramilitary formation) responsible for assassinating Germany's democratically-minded foreign minister Walther Rathenau in 1922. There were a number of Freikorps in the early 1920s. Many of their members went on to become enthusiastic Nazis. The Heimwehr was an Austrian right-wing paramilitary formation, which was responsible for much the same kind of disturbance as the various Freikorps in Germany. May 1 is the International Day of Labor and thus of high significance for Marxist groups. Richard Kunze was a well-known anti-semitic politician in the early Weimar Republic known as Knüppelkunze (Kunze with a club) because he carried a rubber billy club in case he got into an argument.

[2] The vast majority of German fraternities (Burschenschaften) in this period were dueling societies. Only a few, mostly Catholic and Jewish fraternities, eschewed weapons.

bergbund, Tscheka, Feme, Stahlhelm, and Jungdo, all the way to the Cell G and, finally, Hitler. The left is less confusing. It's not so divided, and, somehow, seems to be more serious.

But Elsa, that girl, she has to stick her nose into everything. And she's so young! She can't possibly understand what's going on in the world situation.

"Father, I just want to know what they want." Hmmm. Even as a young child the girl had no patriotism.

"Martha," said Pitt to his wife, admittedly smiling a little at the memory, "do you remember how the wind blew her little white cap off her head at the university library and how she tore right into the middle of a parade of soldiers to get it back? How the soldiers, with their rifles shouldered, just marched over it and pushed her back? How Elsa turned chalk white and shouted at them "Poo on your silly uniforms, I hate you all!" How she balled her little fists and stamped her feet. And you were so afraid that they would bayonet both of you. When it was all over, Elsa stroked her trampled hat over and over. I spanked her after that, but she never said boo and never cried. Martha, do you remember any of this?"

"Now something similar has happened. I know that the Kaiser's gone. It doesn't make sense to spank her anymore. But I was allowed to go and pick her up, your daughter. She just has to go wherever there are barricades! Now, your turn, Elsa, spit it out, but make it snappy. Tell your mother why they arrested you!"

"Papa, stop it! Mama is just getting upset."

"You shouldn't be so contradictory. Out with it, or I'll make you get a move on."

"OK, Mama, it wasn't so bad, but it was interesting. And I was completely right. I'm just walking along, when one of them sticks his rifle into my chest and says, "Halt! Stop right there." I say, "I thought the days of recruits giving orders to civilians were over." Then the man says, "All right. Come along with me." Then he grabbed my arm rudely. Look, here's the bruise. Anyway, he dragged me to his superior officer in the barracks, and that one was as drunk as a skunk."

"Elsa, what kind of language is that for a young girl?"

"Because he was shit-faced instead of just drunk? But Mother, listen, it gets even better. The officer — his men called him Lieutenant — dismissed his soldiers and then asked me for my name, etc. He thought that the name 'Deutsch' sounded Jewish, but my blonde hair and my being Protestant seemed to calm him down. Then he mumbled something about a blacklist. It was clear that he thought I should be on it. Then he said that I should be taken into protective custody, for my own protection of course. He claimed that the Reds had the barracks surrounded. In fact, he said that even he hadn't gone out for days, because he was afraid that they'd shoot him in the back. Then, he grabbed me by the neck and tried to kiss me. Really! I bashed

25

him as hard as I could. Look at my glove; you see how bloody it is? Then he shut the door and came at me like some kind of wild animal. I started screaming for help. He chased me around the room, and when I fell down he stomped me with his boots. Finally the others broke down the door and came in. They took the Herr Officer away, and I was bandaged up and taken to the infirmary. Besides that, they kept apologizing and begging me not to talk about what he did.

But I told them very forcefully that this is a completely unacceptable way to treat a respectable German citizen, dragging me from the street and taking me to a blind drunk who locks me in a room and kicks me. Now I really understand what kind of country these people want. They realized that, and allowed Papa to come get me. Besides the bump on my head, my legs are hurt, too. I haven't even shown you that."

"I think she's telling the truth." said Pitt Deutsch with only a little remaining skepticism. "They were so strangely polite to me and kept asking me to pardon the 'unfortunate occurrences.' I just thought they meant your arrest."

Even though Pitt Deutsch was still a little annoyed with his "scoundrel," he couldn't stop himself from ruffling her hair and declaring: "Elsa, you're a wild one. Martha, where do you think she got that from? Anyway, she sure showed them."

"God, Papa," Elsa snipped, "you know that I've never been able to stand any kind of uniforms. Anyway, there's no reason for you to be so happy that I showed them. I acted the same way they did, so-called 'gentlemen'. They're nothing but reactionaries."

Martha could only sigh: "My God, my God. The scandal. The whole street already knows that you were arrested."

With the words "What's the matter with that?," Elsa hobbled out of the room.

"Children bring nothing but worries," groaned Martha. "And it's not like she's the only thing on my mind, either."

"What else is bothering you?" asked Pitt.

"Something's been going on with Klara for a while. I have a feeling that she's been lying to us about something. In fact, I'm sure that she's keeping something from us. For example, I found a pair of torn men's socks in her dresser. And, lately I've seen her with a young man, who looks like somebody I've seen in your factory."

"Now, Martha, I don't think there's anything to it. Our Klara is a such a good girl. I don't believe she would do anything wrong. I would stick my hand in the fire for her. But the story about the men's socks is odd. I promise I'll look into it."

Herr Deutsch wasn't able to completely clear up the story with his Klara. He would also not have been happy that his Klara, who just a few years before could have had her choice of a whole circle of officers, had her heart set on a simple bookkeeper at his company, who for his part didn't even intend to marry her. No, the young, rather handsome young man didn't want to get married yet, certainly not.

"Besides," thought the young man, "who knows if Klara's father was smart enough to steer his ship through the inflation?" It was nice, though, to have somebody who was always willing to pick up her part of the tab when they went out. She paid more than half for the boat on the lake. She cooked and brought him the food. Klara even came to his room, cleaned up, washed and darned his socks, and sorted his laundry. A young man can use this kind of service. Fair enough, she was a bit controlling, but she had such a pretty smile when she lay beside him in bed. Now, it's true that the Gollnow girl — that little devil — was bubblier, livelier, and had a nicer body. She was a great dancer. In fact, if he sat out a dance somebody else was sure to snap her up. Klara Deutsch, though, did have her advantages. The two, taken together, were perfect. "I just have to be sure that they don't know anything about each other." That's how the young man thought. In fact, that's how a lot of young men think. Klara protected him from Herr Deutsch, who just wouldn't understand.

Klara did have some issues with this young man. One day she saw him with his other girl. Another time she got very upset that he didn't seem to have time for her on Sundays anymore.

He claimed that he was invited somewhere, and he had to go to improve his chances for social advancement. Finally, one last time he really left her in the lurch. "Sweetie, you should have been more careful. How did you think that I could help you? People don't get married for that reason anymore. If every girl who got pregnant got married, there wouldn't be any more single girls, and then single men would have to share."

Klara was horrified. Now a child by this man was the last thing she wanted. She certainly couldn't say anything at home. Herr Deutsch, who swore he would "stick his hand in the fire for her," would kick her out onto the street without a second thought. She immediately started hunting down physicians' addresses. Wedding, Neukölln, the Kurfürstendamm. In the end more than half a dozen doctors. But one was dead; another was abroad; the third said he couldn't do it any more, nowadays they were onto one's tail immediately; the fourth claimed never to have performed one without serious medical reasons. And the other two — probably because Klara had broached the issue awkwardly — kicked her right out, even though she knew for a fact that perfectly healthy women had been to them to be freed of their problems. In a conversation with a girlfriend, ostensibly about nothing, Klara found out about a "wise" woman. As she went to this woman's address and

27

rang her bell, a neighboring door opened, and Klara was hauled into a strange apartment.

"For Christ's sake, Miss, get ya'self in here already, otherwise there will be more trouble. They came and nabbed Schulzie this morning," said the woman, already having shut the door behind her, "and the cops is still snooping around here. Like I always says, there's always more trouble. Stay put for a while, so they'll think you'se here visitin.'"

Klara cried for the first time in a long time. How merciful fate was after all. A few hours earlier and she'd be sitting in prison. The simple woman stroked her face: "Don't cry. Little problems like this happen sometimes. Why hang yer head? Is yer boyfriend outside?"

No, he wasn't.

One night Elsa, who shares a room with Klara, asks quietly, "Klara, what's wrong? Are you having a nightmare?"

"No. I'm just not feeling well. Go back to sleep." "Like a dog," she thinks, "who's about to bite the bullet." Her brothers, her mother: nobody can be allowed to notice anything. Feeling chilly, she walks to the window. The street is empty. It's raining. She feels as if she has thrown her life away and all that's left is an empty shell. She doesn't want to lie down or do anything that might start the others asking questions.

Klara looks tired and old. The incident with the young man has come and gone. Even he is past it. Indeed, from his perspective, once was enough.

Life has a way of making people think about new things. There is panic in the Family Deutsch. The last machines were sold for dollars. The war bonds never did pay off. The government wants Herr Deutsch to pay a special Ruhr fee.[3] Taxes rise while distribution slows to a halt. If Herr Deutsch pays his debts in full, and he does, as he is an honorable man, then he'll have no money for new raw materials. Elsa drops out of the university. The family sells the villa to a foreigner for Czech crowns, but fire sales never bring the real value of what's sold. Herr Deutsch sees his years of hard work melting into nothing. Only the Czech crowns keep him above water, and that only for a little while. Klara and Elsa take jobs as secretaries. But the wages that they bring home barely pay for bread and a quarter pound of butter. Elsa must be very good at this kind of work and very hard working. She is able to land a major position with a major investment firm: she is the sole secretary to the entire directorate. Indeed, she has the same degree of respect and re-

[3] In January 1923, in response to Germany's claim that it was unable to pay war reparations, France sent soldiers to occupy the Ruhr, Germany's industrial region in the West. The German government financially supported Ruhr workers in a policy of passive resistance, and recouped some of the cost from employers.

sponsibility as the firm's purchasing agent. Her youth does make her job difficult at first, but she pulls it out and is even able to ensure that she will be paid every third day.[4]

Klara, on the other hand, lands a job at an automobile firm — cars in Germany are selling like hotcakes to foreigners — but she is badly mistreated. The bosses drive around all day with their customers, totally forgetting about their shop, leaving Klara sitting by the open windows late into the night waiting for them to bring the cars back into the showroom. Only then can the windows be shut. Klara works with the customers, keeps the books, writes the official correspondence, posts the advertisements, and when she has a moment, demonstrates the cars. She learned to drive in the family car, now long since gone. When she is doing this, Werner, the jack-of-all-trades, watches the shop while she drives to the Litzensee or the Reichskanzler Square and back. Klara is quite good at selling cars for hard currency. Swedish crowns and English pounds are the most highly valued. If all of this isn't enough, the owner's wife will drop her two children off to be watched when the serving maid has a day off. Her salary sounds good, but she is paid in marks like before, and only on the last day of the month. It's barely enough for a streetcar ticket. Even as her stomach grumbles, the oil fumes give her a headache. Cranking the car — automatic starters are still rare at this time — puts a lot of strain on her wrists, even as her bosses sit with customers in elegant restaurants in the park, or at the race track, or even in the city, perhaps on the Behren Strasse or Hardenberg Strasse, their stomachs agreeably full of good food and wine. They are Christians, but they don't seem so very Christian to Klara. Their wives can change jewelry as often as others change clothes. They sit by the fountain at the former Masquotte, with pearl tiaras on their heads and diamonds on their hands. Klara both knows this and sees it in the boss's personal bank statement, which she is charged with keeping in order. She, on the other hand, doesn't even get a sales commission. Every morning she is charged with bringing the bosses coffee, butter, white rolls, and various delicacies for breakfast, naturally with port wine. Sometimes she's tasked with taking their personal mail to their houses. She has stopped doing that, though, after the unfortunate "boxing match" between herself and the boss. He responded by threatening to fire her, but as of yet he has no replacement for Klara.

Klara knows, however, that it's only a matter of time.

---

[4] Hyperinflation in Germany was so severe, that the exchange rate of marks to the dollar reached 4,200,000,000,000 to 1 in November 1923. Thus workers wanted to be paid as frequently as possible so that their wages could almost keep up with rising prices.

There are fireworks when Klara finally does leave. It's a good thing, too, that most members of the Family Deutsch are made of tough stuff. They can handle with a quiet conscience much that would have others in an uproar. A few weeks after the firm's chief appealed to Klara's femininity, he demanded a thorough review of the books.

"Books" is right. In fact, Klara instituted the only accounting this firm had ever had. When she asked for the books, all she was given were two primitive school composition books. She was never able to get the boss to submit receipts for all of his various withdrawals from the till. It was simply impossible. Klara certainly protested having to preside over such loose accounting for the business. The only response she ever got was:

"Get over it, little lady. We take care of recording the large withdrawals ourselves, and the little ones have always gone without any documentation. But, if it makes you happy, then give me a quick fifty and write it in your book! I don't have time for receipt keeping."

Fifty marks three times a day wasn't unusual. Down payments for cars — only in hard currency, of course — also often made their way into the boss's pocket. Often the till didn't have even enough cash for postage or to pay the messengers their weekly wages.

This system would unquestionably have driven a lesser person crazy.

Pitt Deutsch, though, had raised his children, especially the four older ones, in the proper and strict manner. They didn't just look spic and span on the outside, as Berliners used to say, clean, well groomed, and in order. Pitt Deutsch had also given each of them a strong character. The four oldest would have been the most dedicated civil servants any state could ever wish for. The Ten Commandments of Lutheranism had been explained to them with more than a few swats, and were fully part of their beings. Only with Jürgen had this strength of character not fully "taken."

And now a man had the nerve to sit there and say:

"What is this fifty marks all about? I never got it. This either, little lady. And who did you buy port wine for? I never drank so much port. You're saying that I took the hundred Swedish Crowns down payment? Are you crazy, little lady. Now, where's the money? Hand it over!"

Klara is certainly not crazy. With a temporary calm she reminded him: "This time and that, when you wanted it, I gave you the cash. Don't you remember anymore?"

He refuses to accept her explanation.

At this point Klara can't be rattled. Her salary is just enough to cover her transportation for a month. She is stuck sitting behind a desk, in a corner location that is certainly very pretty with its five display windows, from early morning until late at night. Angrily she bangs her fist onto the table and shouts:

"You think you can convince me that I took the money that you pocketed? When you make me give your girlfriend cash from the till? I'm going to call my father's lawyer and ask if he will take this as a defamation case. Just say that you don't want me as an employee anymore because I won't sleep with you! You've already threatened me with that. Whatever you do, though, don't accuse innocent people, Herr Wilna!"

"Did you hear that, Dörre?" the boss called over to his partner, who, for a change, is actually at work. Ha! That's a laugh! Every word a lie! As if I would go to bed with this silly goose! That would have really been all I needed! You have quite an imagination, little lady!"

"I see," Klara sneered, cool sarcasm in her voice. "Then perhaps I should remind you why you have a bandage on your chin and why you only opened the door that you shut behind me when I grabbed the telephone and shouted 'I'm being attacked' into it. It would be easy to have this verified by the telephone service and the police!"

With this, Klara packed her possessions and asked for her salary.

At home, Deutsch spent a long time considering whether the bosses should be taken to court. But that would cost money, and money was getting shorter all the time.

"Yeah," added Peter. "Even honor is a financial question, now."

Elsa's assessment is much brasher. "Who cares what a jerk like that thinks about Klara. The most important thing is what we know and what we think is important."

Max suggests going over with Peter and giving Wilna a proper thrashing (and Dörre too, in the bargain). That character has rankled him for a good, long time.

Peter is a chemistry student. He has had to change his dissertation topic a few times, though, since the chemicals that he needs for his experiments aren't yet available in Germany again. This is quite upsetting for his advisor, Privy Councillor Professor Thomas, as Peter is one of his favorite students.

The student body is composed of rather mature-looking men. The professor has just the right touch for this unusual group. They arrive in their well-worn uniforms. They work together and help each other, without any regard for religious differences. Even foreigners are back, including students from far-flung China. Much about them astonishes the locals, not least their gray silk robes and their very fluent German. English exchange students trade war stories with the others. It's as if they hadn't been shooting at each other such a short time ago.

Frau Martha spends her time lamenting her personal bank account, which has gone to nothing.

Max, in his first semester at the university studying economics, races to Neukölln with a few Czech crowns, because butchers there are still selling meat at yesterday's prices but giving today's exchange rate for the crowns. That could mean as much as an extra pound of meat. America is sending vast quantities of frozen meat. Civil servants, who are paid their salaries in advance, if they are smart, are in a great position to buy up some inventory. But not all are so clever. Many heads of households won't allow next month's money to be spent on this month's expenses.

Finally, the currency is so inflated that it has to be double printed and looks to all the world like a bus ticket.[5]

Herr Deutsch's creditors force him to sell off his machines for a song — but in American dollars. The government refuses to believe that he has fallen into poverty and impounds the rest to pay his back taxes. Their living space shrinks; only the children grow.

The needy years flow by in their monotonous way. Pitt can't find a way to earn a living, but spends money in continuing to look. And Martha is hard at work in the house, because the expenses need to drop. In fact, she's working harder than she ever did as a house servant.

It shouldn't be particularly surprising that our man Deutsch, to whom the glory of the imperial era gave the strength for such tireless work, who gladly subsumed all of his own celebrations to birthdays and burials of Kaisers past, and who then saw all of it disappear under the present circumstances, for which he holds the Republic completely responsible, that this man, who believes that Germany and the Kaiser should be one and the same thing, hates the Germany of his children.

For him, the slaps in the face and terrible insults occurring in the Reichstag cannot replace the laughing, festive street that was Unter den Linden. For him it's no better than a fraud that the snappy military tones of the pre-war era — a time in which each and every sergeant-major saw himself as an autocratic god — are now a thing of the past. Certainly Pitt thinks that the new police are politer than their blue-uniformed predecessors; "But still" he says, "there are murders in the streets. In the Reichstag and in the Landtag, which really ought to be honorable houses for superior, calmly deliberative men, rogues run around slandering people and fighting like cats and dogs.[6] My God, and we're supposed to be a people proud of our freedom. They're treating each other like lepers and forgetting the most basic rules of decorum."

"Martha, don't you see it, too?" As we can see, Herr Deutsch is talking with his wife rather more again. "Is everything as fouled up as it seems to

[5] During the inflation, the currency devalued so quickly that the bills would often have the old value crossed out and printed over with a newer, significantly higher, denomination.

[6] The Landtag was the Prussian state parliament.

me? Even if they don't have any political insight, can't young people at least show a little discipline? We don't have anything decent to eat. We have to sell anything that isn't bolted down. It's not just that we've lost our faith. We've lost so much more than anybody else has. We had to climb down again, bitterly, and I'm no better off than I was thirty-five years ago when I came back to Berlin. I even did a great service to the Fatherland, in my way. What did we get for that? But are we bothering anybody just because the world's falling apart? Because things are going badly, are we smashing out other people's windows? Are we stealing? Are we committing murder? Do we have to add that to all the other misery? Weren't most people — not us — even hungrier during the war? But people knew then that breaking shop windows wouldn't make things any better. And today? Even if all the gold in the world was divided up, it wouldn't last for a year. They'd have to divide the whole world itself up and then give it out equally. Instead they're choking us, burning our crops when they're growing too well, and letting the people go hungry."

CHAPTER FOUR

NOW, TO DISCUSS THE FOURTEENTH YEAR AFTER THE END

FOURTEEN YEARS HAVE PASSED since the end of the war.

The gramophone whines on an early morning: "We'd be good, and not so rough, if only circumstances weren't so tough."[1]

Max shouts through the door, "Turn off that damned noise box! I'm so sick of 'we would be gooood!' We're crude and without feeling from the start. With little understanding, and don't add to what we do have. You let your sympathy be aroused by a few fur-coated socialists. It's only a song. You should have been at the Institute for Politics yesterday. Then you would have seen how far gone these youngsters, these unripe radishes, are. They don't understand anything — and their 'will to be gooood'! Bullshit! It's not even political. They're only political on the surface; behind that they're just hyenas, barking out the parties's songs."

Klara mediates, as usual: "Fine. Just put on another record. Let's not fight about politics again."

Her good will is for nothing, however. Her brothers and sisters just start shouting at each other again: "Maybe 'Green is the heath, the heath is green' or 'The Danube's pleasant waves'?"

From a behind a pile of books in the corner, Peter, at 31 the second oldest but still the quietest of the siblings, almost whispers: "vivere non necesse est — if people could only hear you. It's not worth it for a fighting horde to live and sacrifice itself over and over again, like the ancients did. No one has any respect for anyone else, and nineteen-year-olds are writing off even those only five or ten years older. No, it's not worth being alive."

"Then just drop dead, old boy. You'll have the thanks of a grateful Fatherland."

Susi yells at this last, especially crude, brother. "Somebody really ought to give it to you, Jürgen. You're just an upstart, wet behind the ears, too lazy

---

[1] These lines come from the end of act 1, scene 3 of Bertolt Brecht and Kurt Weill's *Threepenny Opera*.

to work, but happy to take our money and then be a jerk. Your family feeling is getting on my nerves. I'm going out."

"Say hello to your boyfriend and bring me home some money!"

Susi simply adds, "Jürgen, the born pimp," carefully touches up her wind-blown hair, tosses a funny little thing on her head that's trying to be a cap, pastels her face, and paints a sweet little cherry onto her lips. Short jacket, tight little behind — and the men on the street follow her with their eyes and run the tips of their tongues lightly over their lips.

With his hands in his pockets, as if he wanted to pull his belt down over his narrow hips, Jürgen circles her and adds, "If I were a banker like him, you'd be my lover, too."

Susi walks past him like he doesn't exist, waves to Max and Klara, and runs her hand through Peter's hair as she passes through the door. Then, in an instant, she has put her family out of her mind. At least that's how it would appear to some.

Klara, at 32 years old, her nerves shot, thinks a lot about her family's rise and fall, muses on the war and other recent history, stares at the door that Susi has just walked through and wonders why she can't take life as lightly as her sister does. Only ten years separate the sisters, but that ten years is a whole world. Well, is it really a whole world? Susi has her own peculiarities, odd moments in which one can tell that this young Susi both knows and sees more than she will admit to. Then she seems to line up with the older siblings and has, suddenly, a very old face. But when Susi walks along the street, she's young, bubbly, and fascinating. When Klara gets together with other people, she only feels old and estranged. She has less of an understanding of today's youth than does her mother. Mother simply isn't going to worry about it. In the end, she is a much more basic person.

Then there is Elsa. Only two years separate them, but Klara understands Elsa even less than she understands Susi. Elsa is very smart and has been quite successful at work. She never speaks about her private life at home, though. She has lived through all the same circumstances as Klara has — the family's glory and subsequent crash, the war, inflation, and putsches. Yet, even though she's only two years younger than Klara is, she looks so young and attractive. Even though she earns less now than she did just a few years ago, and has a harder time earning it than Susi does, she makes more out of the limited free time she has, and her efforts to appear ageless are successful. Elsa has experienced the dos and the don'ts of her time. She is certainly the cleverer of the two older sisters. She uses various tools to fight against creeping time, and always manages to appear up-to-date. Secretly, though, Elsa has the same suspicion of younger people that they have of their elders. With a cold, calculating eye, she engages in the same tomfoolery as they do, merely in order to give herself an inner feeling of superiority.

Elsa is surrounded by a wide variety of men, various because none of them is really sure exactly what makes her tick. Characteristic for Elsa is their range of races, religions, and professions. Elsa is international in the broadest sense of the term. One sees her as a lover, the next, a motherly woman, a third thinks of her as a colleague, a fourth seeks her out for advice on tricky work and marriage questions. If some call her sexless, others find her to be sensuous. Views on her appearance and character are just as varied. Many see her as a proud, elegant lady. Others are amazed at what a warm human being she is, not proud at all. Elsa must be some sort of a master of living, as she is for each man that which he wants to see in her. She must have descended from Aspasia.[2] The practical sense that she is blessed with makes her even cleverer than her brother Peter, and therefore the smartest one in her family. Despite this — or precisely because of it — Elsa's life is not simple.

Even as Klara was giving such considerable thought to the question of Elsa, the latter came home and walked into the room.

"Home" wouldn't be quite right, as Elsa had lived for several years in a "furnished" apartment, and had only recently gotten her own place.

She sat down with Max to ask him about the previous night's student forum. "Was it an interesting evening?" A tacit understanding had developed between these two siblings that allowed them to share with each other what interested each of them most.

Max, generally one to engage in lively debate, could only answer wearily, "You know, it was supposed to address the question, 'Where does today's student stand?' It became something totally different, though. Almost none of the speakers from the various parties held to the topic. All of them, regardless of party, started by saying, 'I'm not going to speak for my organization, my party tonight, am not authorized to, but. . . .' And then the rest was party propaganda."

"That's not so odd. Young people today cover their tracks more than they used to. After all, all the parties are appealing to them."

"But Elsa, that's not what's bothering me. I'm perfectly able to handle some lack of discipline. I could look away, too, if this was the so-called 'flower of the nation' that was determined to show its intellectual side. No, something else was going on here."

"You're full of it." With this Jürgen decided to join the conversation. "We are disciplined. The Führer teaches us discipline."

---

[2] Aspasia, the consort of Pericles in fifth-century BCE Athens, was well known as a conversationalist and for having an interesting mind. Many ancient writers also claimed that she was a courtesan and brothel keeper.

"Then I wonder why your Führer supports the stupid things that you do," interjected Elsa.

"The Führer stands by us, and we stand by the Führer. We don't ever abuse the Führer's trust," Jürgen shouted, his face bright red to his temples.

"Boy, quiet down," answered Elsa, keeping her composure. "We're not deaf. Here's the one thing I want to say to you: I don't believe that you are all just tools in the hand of your Führer. There are many unpredictable elements in your organization that are going to turn around and bite you."

"Elsa, we don't waver. We know what we're doing. We're Germans, after all!"

"My dear, what are we, just annoying foreigners? Some people want to copyright 'German' like they invented it! Now be a good boy and leave us alone."

"I am leaving. Paul understands me better than you do."

Elsa, jeeringly: "I believe, my dear, that soon you'll be as arrogant as he is!"

A slamming door shook the entire house.

"You see," Elsa said to Max, "he didn't want to hear that. Heaven forbid anybody say anything about his sweet young thing, Paul Jones, the actor with the hang-dog face."

She knew a number of National Socialists and understood their point of view. What she really didn't like, though, were boys like her brother Jürgen and Paul Jones. Paul Jones was an alias for an unemployed actor who now and again gave free public recitals. One day he'd be driving a car, the next he'd be in editorial offices begging for a free lunch. Jones was a mysterious character who seemed to make himself at home anywhere he went. He swung both ways, hugging girls with his skinny arms, yet on top of that was what Berliners called a "sweet" boy. His influence on Jürgen was catastrophic. Jürgen wasn't a bad kid, but he had fallen in with the wrong crowd.

"So Max, now that it's quiet, please tell me more about what today's students are thinking."

"The whole evening came and went and nobody told us where today's student stands. He doesn't stand. He doesn't sit. He just seems to hover. He's also remarkably less mature than we were five or ten years ago. But he's proud to be a proletarian, . . . at least that's what these people said. Now, I was just in a meeting of young workers that was attended by some white-collar types too, and I have to say that they seemed much more solid and self-possessed than the university boys did yesterday."

"Max, that's because the workers don't see their proletarianism as shameful, but want to raise its social status. I think they're envisioning an improved middle class. The students, on the other hand, seem to come from two groups. Some are out of the pre-war middle class with eccentric views, and some are from the working-class circles that don't value manual labor anymore. It's just like our mother wanted it: we went to university and our brothers didn't learn father's trade or any other practical skill. The one group is broke and thinks that because they're poor, they're now proletarian. The other one wants to work for a proletarian revolution."

"Sure, but everyone wants to get ahead, Elsa," interjects Max.

"Of course! But getting ahead doesn't just mean getting into professions that are already too full. Instead it should be a kind of self-confidence about one's work, whatever that work is."

"Sure, and a lot of them who have a small but secure state grant call themselves proletarians and don't hesitate to join student worker organizations, which involve themselves in politics, especially in the border areas, taking bread and work away from real proletarians."[3]

"Everything has two sides. But people just want to look at one of them. It's an upside-down world, too. People who can barely eke out a living want to go to university. They think it's the only way to get ahead in the world. But the lords of this earth, whose children could freely and without worry attend university, mostly prefer to stick their kids in practical training for a career, because they have little regard for theoretical knowledge."

"But I'll bet these young people see themselves as being responsible," said Elsa.

"Of course. And the younger they are, the bigger they talk. That's just the way it is today. I heard a nineteen-year-old say, 'Today we're nothing. We sit in the hostels until 4:00, and then we wander the streets until 12:00, because somebody else has our bed until 10:00. And anyway we can't sleep forever. We're out of work, and we don't even want to work. Yet we're still going to be the ones to turn the world upside down and build a new social class!'"

After she'd thought for a while, Elsa said, "I'll bet that soon we'll see a new kind of socialism, because this kind of big talk won't make the real workers, the ones who use their brains and hands, very happy."

It was unusual for Elsa to state her views so clearly, even to her brother Max.

Max broke the silence. "Funny, I was thinking something similar yesterday. I put it like this: one shouldn't have one's sole source of pride in being proletarian and portraying the middle class as something absolutely

---

[3] "Border areas" probably refers to those areas in East Prussia and Pomerania bordering on the newly reconstituted Poland. Poland was partitioned among Russia, Prussia, and Austria in the late eighteenth century, and only came back into existence after the First World War. Part of the territory of this new Poland was taken from Germany. Many Germans remained unreconciled to this in the interwar era, and spoke of Germany's "bleeding frontiers."

worthless. We've seethed and fought over this for too long already. What we should do is work harder to cultivate ourselves the way we used to. But instead, on the one hand, the Germans have been overexploiting our old cultural goods for too long; on the other, they want to fob off as good for everyone one-sided ideals that have nothing at all to do with culture. Here again, we're showing no respect to our ancestors."

"Max, what I think is that the historical ups and downs that are visible in both small and large oscillations in the past, both in economic and cultural terms, are going to spread to our era too. This time the seismic tremors are bigger, and the quakes aren't as isolated, but there will be a way out. I also think that young people will find it."

Max was filled again with admiration for his sister's belief in human reason and faith in mankind's moral mission.

Jürgen returns home, looking very pale, and they stop their conversation immediately. Elsa asks him whether his wife wasn't home, or if she was in a bad mood.

As an answer Jürgen smashes a coffee cup.

"But Jürgen," intones Klara, who had been quietly sitting and darning socks in the rather bare room, "where will we find money to buy a new one?" She then begins to collect the shards.

"Cut the crap! Always the same implied criticism: Why don't you have a job? First get a job, bring home some money, then you can smash some cups? I'm sick of this! I can't stand it anymore!"

Peter takes this last complaint seriously. "Jürgen! Nobody said anything like that. You're imagining things. None of the six of us have a decent job. How could we accuse you of anything?"

"Hey, listen. The old man always says that if he wasn't so old, he'd find a job."

"That's because Father just doesn't understand the way things are today. He just can't see that we're already considered too old to get hired, too."

"That's easy or you to say. You went to university. You'll land something for sure."

"Don't be so sure, Jürgen. I did really well in my studies, and still, for years, couldn't find a position as a chemist. Then, I thought I could take the pharmacy exam and at least get a job at an apothecary. Now you see I haven't found anything there either. And I'm even out of unemployment benefits. If it weren't Elsa and Susi, where would we be? But whatever you do, don't blame me if you couldn't learn anything."

"Not just couldn't, but didn't want to, either," Klara adds angrily. "He was too dumb for all the schools he went to. He was too 'fine' to work with his hands. Too weak for sports. Now, one thing he could do is grow long

Chinese fingernails and play the lord and master at the baths. Furthermore, you can't even trust his politics. Sometimes he'll support Avalov, sometimes Hitler — a real patriot.[4] With a toothbrush and a roll in his pocket he'll go to Argentina. Then he'll send a telegram that says 'send money or I'll starve.' That's just like him. A cheap little adventurer, that's all he is. He took our last bit of money, and even the word 'scoundrel' is too good a description for him."

"For God's sake, shut up you stupid cow. If you could just have gotten married, you wouldn't have to see me anymore."

"Do you hear how fresh he is, on top of everything else?" With this, Klara starts to cry.

"Children, don't fight. Klara, there's no point dredging all of this up again."

"I'm the one who's dredging things up?" Now Klara is really angry. "He's right about one thing. I don't want to see this jerk anymore. Why did Father have to sell our piano? For this brat's debts at the fancy food stores. For those crabs, lobsters, and I don't know what else. Why did we have to sell our last carpet? Because our 'baron' decided to buy his friend a gramophone console. I could go on for hours. What a perfect good-for-nothing."

Jürgen is ready to jump on Klara, but the others get between them and lead Klara out, shaking and in tears. Klara is already old and used up before her time. Her brothers and sisters know this, and enfold her with sympathy. She doesn't have the slightest chance of finding a job. Nobody could blame a boss who decided to hire a younger, less nervous, and cheaper girl. But the situation at home is so tense, so ready to explode that it's hard for all of them to be calm instead of running out, screaming, into the street.

Their mother doesn't provide them with any security. When conflict flares up among them, all she ever says is: "If you don't like it, then go!" That's why the siblings always try to sort out their problems among themselves, making amends if they can. Because of this, Elsa feels especially guilty about the scene with Jürgen, and tries to bring a little peace back into the family. She's especially happy, then, when Susi shows up, arms laden with packages. Susi, beaming, starts to unpack. Her excited audience is transfixed like children at the circus. Even as her little hat flies onto the bed that's scrunched into the room, and a few errant flowers fall off the table, the newly unpacked package produces some wonderful treats. Susi takes the opportunity to cross-examine her brothers and sisters. "What did you eat today?" "Pork and beans!" "What did you eat yesterday?" "Potato soup, no sausage!"

---

[4] Pavel Bermondt-Avalov was an adventurer and a general in the White Army during the Russian Civil War.

"What are you planning on eating tomorrow?"

"Beans without bacon rinds? Enough already. Why the interrogation? When there's nothing at all, these don't sound quite so bad."

"My dears, I have good news. Here comes three days of high living. To-morrow we're off to the movie . . . all of us! Now you can open your eyes." Miracle of miracles, there's a leg of mutton, a sausage as thick as your arm, ham, butter, even a loaf of white bread.

"I have to say," begins Jürgen . . .

"Boy, I'm not going to talk to you. I know how you gush, but I'd rather you not; instead, eat up!"

Amazing what a well-set table will do for everybody's mood. They start to banter, laughing and fighting about what movie they should see tomor-row. Elsa sends Helmut, the baby, out to get some beer.

Max is the first to speak. "Children, I just want to say that when we ate like this every day, it never tasted so good." With this, Susi doles out some spending money, and Elsa distributes everybody's allowance.

Peter says that something about this just isn't right. Max responds, "Just give me a chance. I'll have a great idea, then we'll all be on easy street."

"Alright Mr. Economist, just what kind of idea are you waiting on. Maybe one that will bail Germany out?"

With this, they all settle down on the balcony, and Elsa is seized by a lyrical mood. "If it's OK with all of you, I'd like to recite a 'modern' poem." They laugh and shout: "Give it to us, oh great, old poet! Who knew we had a genius in the family. Shoot. But if it's sad, we ain't gonna cry, and that's a promise."

With this, Elsa starts:

> "Listen! The trolley speeds by,
>   Like a flaming chain, burning bright.
>   We live high up,
>   Under the roofs of Berlin
>   Because the rent is steep.
>
> The fresh air
> And the swallow's chirp under the roofline is our reward.
> Think of it, in the middle of the city!
>
> Now a D-train hurtles onward to some distant land.
> A lord from afar
> — Tomorrow he'll be sunning his bare skull —
> Sits unashamed with two women.
>
> The poverty in the dwellings he passes
> Charitably hidden by closed blinds.
> But next door,

Two sons, burnt brown,
Deal skat with their father.
Yes, that's here, too.

Further along a young woman
— her day job's in some office—
Cleans windowpanes deep into the evening.

Such is life in the five-story buildings
Stuck between the train tracks.
The families, fighting and laughing, on their balconies.
Seldom any solitude.

A child, a dog, a radio blaring,
Further on, the subway thunders,
And a compressor moans.

High above, a cool May breeze blows.
Waldmeister streams out of a bowl.
I see a colorful floor mat
And throw myself down.
The cactus with its odd knots,
Hortensias blooming, blue and red.
The wild wine, shot into the skies
With nothing to stop it.

The clothesline swings happily.
Rain sprays from the balcony at 11:00
Dampening the whole 'splendor'.

Heavens wide, stars shining bright.
In between, fireworks crack.
The moon laughing as a hundred years before:
La fortune comme la lune!
A song rises from the street:
Yesterday the Marseillaise,
Today the "Horst-Wessel-Lied"[5]

On the ground floor, two whisper of love.
A fawn hangs over this self-same door.

---

[5] This was one of the most popular of the Nazis' songs, dedicated to the memory of Horst Wessel, a pimp killed in an altercation with Communists whom Josef Goebbels, Hitler's propaganda genius, was able to turn into a martyr of the Nazi cause.

The stamp of the policemen's feet rings in quiet.
But it can't cloak the despondency.
Be quiet! Hush!
The neighbors can hear you.
Go to a party. Announce yourselves.
We are not free.
Not even on the balcony.

"Oh Elsa!" came the cries from the peanut gallery. "You really are a poet. Why not write it down? Elsa, I don't have a clue about poetry, but this captured everything perfectly."

"Kids, don't be silly! Write it down! Even if it had merit, who reads anything like this today? Who has the time, or the patience? The unemployed have the time, but I'll bet they'd toss it out even if it fell into their hands. Nobody deals in dragonfly wings and rose dust, which I know doesn't mean that sentimentality of a certain kind is not still alive. But don't think for one minute that even people as hardened as we are don't, sometimes, even in the middle of the smoke and dust. . . .

Hmmm. A fresh smell of hay, or a strong ruffling sea breeze! Instead of smoke and dust in the air, and a cigarette to calm you down . . . to run once more in open fields, to really be tied to the earth. To walk once more under the fir trees when streaks of sunlight penetrate to the cool, fragrant forest floor. We all know how beautiful Germany is. Imagine, just for a minute, no machines, not having to figure out whether there's enough money to get through the month. To just lie on your back and look at the sky. Just once, to lose yourself and then find yourself again! Then, a real, deep peace in the land. Nobody staring at the other anymore thinking, 'And what party are you with?'"

"Why don't you go down to the Wannsee, to a swimming beach, or to one of the tent cities at the Müggelsee. There you'd get plenty of green, water, and fresh air. The area we live in is gorgeous." With this, "the little one," Helmut, the youngest of the siblings, weighed in.

"You're absolutely right. It is beautiful. Still, all the crowds bother me. See what I mean? The anxiety, the sweat of work that is unloaded there. Don't you get it? Sometimes people don't want to be animals in a herd."

This made no sense to Helmut. "No, I don't get it. That runs completely against my belief in camaraderie. I'm only happy when we're all lying together in our tents and know that all the others will celebrate Sunday together, sticking together even in the bad times."

Peter took this very seriously. "But wait and see for how long. Caged animals who get hungry eventually eat each other."

No. Helmut doesn't want to be anything but a herd animal. "You all want to know something?," says Susi, "what I don't like about this part of town is how fake people are. For example, go to the Wannsee and you'll see girls who are sweet, pretty nothings. Their hair looks terrific. Their makeup is perfect. They have long eyelashes. And everything else is just right, too. So, where do they get the money for this? Now, I don't really care. But, I agree with Elsa that the overpaid jerks should be cut loose — they're a burden on all of us."

"Now Susi, aren't you one of those overcompensated people, always on the move? Besides, you look more like some movie star than like a normal person with two legs."

"My dear Max, you're certainly right. If a girl doesn't go along with the times, then the men, who always seem to want one type for a 'friend' and another for their wife, but still want a lot from both, will just toss her into the trash. And bosses, who shouldn't care in the least about the way their employees look, as long as they are smart, have the same demanding requirements. So many girls who can't pull it off just end up on the streets. But, our salaries aren't high enough for us to be chic. Today you have to look perfect to even get your foot in the door. Fair enough. We understand that. After all, who wants to be left behind? But then we hear the whispers, 'Women today are so ambitious.'"

"In Hollywood," adds Helmut, proud of himself for having read the latest magazine, "they say that thousands barely eat or don't eat at all in order to be able to get their hair done."

"Not just in Hollywood, little one. That competition goes on everywhere. For anyone to have a chance to win, the government should pay for all of us to get made up and have our hair styled."

"Come on, Susi. All you have to do is give your beautician's bill to your Uncle Otto. Then you'll have money *en gros*."

"Oh, Jürgen, with you it never ends, like hay in a haystack, like sand in the desert, . . . you ape! If it were so easy, would we be sitting here now? Is the word 'banker' magic to you? Leave my Otto alone. I go out with him because I like him, not because he helps me out, and helps you out too. I'm not interested in the young bucks, who are obsessed with political organizations, talk big, and always contradict themselves. Otto says half as much in a year as one of them says in a month. And he's not melodramatic when he talks, either. But what he says has weight. Two years ago he told me what kind of mess the economy would be in today. Besides, he doesn't have nearly as much money as you think. It's thanks to his foresight, hard work, and thrift — and his big heart — that he's able to help us. If there's another Black Friday or a new July 13th, he won't have much more to lose. Otto says that if things in Germany don't get better soon, nobody will be able to help anyone out any longer. And the government won't be able to do anything, either."

"Hey Susi, how come you don't have a regular job. Otto could easily find you a position. The little bit of writing you do for him doesn't count as real work. Besides, with your good looks and your youth you could easily find something better."

"What we think, Peter, is that if a man can help to support a woman, then this woman shouldn't take a job from a woman who doesn't have a provider. Old-fashioned, eh? I think that hard work is a good thing, but double dipping today is just wrong."

"You're right!" Klara tosses in. "For example, take that couple of druggists who live above us. They both have good jobs in drugstores. But here sits Peter with his two degrees and he can't find a job at all. He's wearing his fingers to the bone applying for jobs as far away as in Switzerland and England. Couldn't those two get by on his four hundred marks? That's a good salary!"

"Oh well," Peter excuses his colleagues, "with their extra money they can buy more things and in doing so provide income for others. But I would like to see some sort of law that made two-income households illegal. I know that indirectly it would hit the government, because some people would be driven to apply for unemployment. But those people who can depend on somebody for help shouldn't cling to the view that 'if others are getting unemployment, then why shouldn't we?' No! There's no love of country, no matter what form of government is in place, in taking money you don't deserve. But the country has no love for the citizens either if bureaucracy pays people who don't really need the help or fails to pay those who do."

Elsa decides that life in the family Deutsch is quite interesting today, disregarding a couple of minor incidents, that is. Everybody is getting things off their chest.

"You see, Peter" she says "there are maybe a couple of percent who agree with you. And what does that show? Only that in Germany there are more unemployed than are on the lists. And the government isn't very helpful to these conscientious few, either. As thanks for saving it some money, it just trips them up. If your unemployment isn't made official with stamps, records, etc, the welfare office won't give you any of the help that the officially jobless get *eo ipso*. The state will keep your tax assessment high, and you'll have great difficulty proving that you can't pay. You get no reductions, no credits, and the welfare office only looks at you when they find you half starved on the street."

"Or maybe you're like me," chimed in Klara, "and left your job because the bosses made your life a living hell, and you refused to play their games.

Then you can wait and wait until you're half starved. But now the whole world is upside down. It used to be something shameful — unless of course your company went under or was laying off staff — to be let go. Everybody knew that something was wrong with you, and if you had any decency you'd manage. Today decency is punished, and people who are fired are considered to be privileged. Today you'll get state money if you've been fired, even if the reasons that you give for the firing aren't true. But, if would rather you sell your last possession than be a burden to the state, then nobody will believe you. People think that nobody could be such an idiot."

Jürgen pondered this. "Sometimes, we're not so far apart from each other in our opinions. The Führer recently denounced much the same thing."

"You see, we're Germans too? Funny, huh? That we can have the same ideas as your Führer? We can even agree on the little things. Maybe he's shown you the way out of this, too? I'm sure whoever comes to power always overlooks some grievances. Otherwise everything would have been perfect before the war, when the depression hadn't happened. Unfortunately that wasn't the case. Ask Pitt Deutsch. For a while it was only his ideals that kept him afloat."

Peter picked up again, "What you were saying a little bit ago about two-income families . . ."

"Extra, extra!" Susi shouted, "it takes a damned long time for Petey to get the point. OK little one, shoot!"

"You shouldn't always call me Petey, and besides, what kind of language is that? 'Damn'? — You can do better."

"Hard words for hard times. That's why workers speak better German today."

"Fine. Here's what I think. There's something that's always annoyed me. It's a new term, 'work-students'. But you know what? A lot of them are double dippers too. I find it completely unnecessary that if somebody's father is a postmaster, then his son — who's at the university — gets a job as postal assistant, in other words as a 'work student'. A postmaster can support his son at university without taking away somebody else's job. Exactly the same thing happened with another student I knew. The father had a good business. The son became the secretary to the head of a major insurance company. Strings were pulled and the 'young gentleman' got a salary of 420 marks and a schedule of half and whole days off, perfect so that he could go to the meetings of his fencing fraternity, prepare for his exams, and to sleep off his hangovers. I mean, is this really necessary? Doesn't a business have to say, 'we can't do that without annoying too many people?' And, this doesn't even have anything to do with the fact that a really good person in this job would only have to be paid 250 marks. And so there were many in my class who stole somebody else's bread and then were proud to call themselves work-students: they wore elegant clothes, belonged to a fraternity, sat in the pub in the evenings getting tanked up and singing drinking songs with their buddies."

"Peter, don't get so worked up. It's not like you can change it. Of course it's still going on today, too. People with connections stick together. The money they give to the fraternities and spend at the pubs they'll get back a hundred times over. Don't you remember your first few years in the university and the fencing club? The ones who were in it then were pretty hardworking, and still got arrested for their nonsense. Today they're famous, well-paid men in their various organizations. Corps spirit! Honored brother. It wouldn't be so bad if one of us had this kind of situation."

"Fair enough, Elsa, but still, one shouldn't act as if the situation of today's students as a whole has changed completely. Certainly there are more poor people today who want to study, but don't even have enough to eat. There have always been people like that, but they didn't used to make such a big deal of themselves. For example, think about Gärger with his forty marks a month and how, between semesters, he used to work unloading boats in East Prussia. Or think about Vicunna, who would go to the factory at 6:00 A.M., start studying at 3:00, and was as thin as a rake. Or think about Olga, who froze her hands working in the lard factory and unloading boxes on Alexanderplatz and tutored in the afternoons. The poor girl worked her fingers to the bone! And what does she have to show for her meager life and her attempt to improve it? Is her Ph.D. any help to her as a member of a work crew, clearing clumps of grass from the streets, just trying to make enough not to starve or take welfare?"

"What will she do now?" Elsa asked.

"I ran into her recently, carrying the want ads. She'd like a job that will let her use her mind more than clearing clumps of grass with a pickaxe, even though that pays better than teaching children does. But nobody will hire her, poor thing. She was dressed in rags."

Meanwhile, Helmut has decided he would like to go to the ball fields. At least that's what he says.

Elsa looks at him skeptically. "Are you crazy, little man? Max is already going to bed and you want to go play ball? It's too dark to see anything. Have you finished your homework? You know you have to do that before anything else.

"Homework? Come off it!"

"Helmut!" Susi joins in, not completely without justification. "Listen up. There's something fishy about your always wanting to go to the ball fields and never finishing your homework. I'm just going to say one thing. If in six weeks you flunk and have to be held back again, Elsa and I aren't paying your school fees anymore. This just can't go on. It's like with Jürgen all over again. Your teachers tell us that you're capable of good work, but you can't be bothered. Only your P.E. teacher is happy with your work. Mark my words, young man: if this is how you're going to deal with school, you can forget about ever becoming a sailor!"

As she is finishing up this well-intentioned speech, Susi, to lend emphasis to her words, straightens her younger brother's tie and grabs his jacket by the lapels. With a shocked, "What?" she looks at a small cut on her finger. While she runs her tongue over it, she mutters, "Get back over here, you!" and turns over the lapel that she scratched herself on.

The Deutsch children's quiet family discussion erupts again into anger. Susi, you see, is very impulsive. With a "Hmmm! I should have known!" she slaps the almost-grown youth in the face.

Her siblings just look at her, both shocked and curious. The only one who has anything to say is a half-awake Max: "We seem to be a rather quick-witted family. What's wrong this time?"

"What's wrong?," Susi cries, enraged. "Not that he's wearing a hidden swastika pin, but that the rascal has anything to do with politics — still wet behind the ears, constantly failing his classes, nothing but sports on the brain — but politics! Somebody should beat the living daylights out of this kid."

"What do you mean, 'kid'?," Helmut countered. "I know as much about politics as you do, understand? Everyone in my class belongs to the Party. If the principal turned all of our lapels over, he'd see how useless it is to try and stop us."

"I see. So, you're happy to take money from a state that you've set yourself against. Immoral to the core."

"Wake up. Whoever takes advantage of the state weakens it too, and that's what we want to do."

"But Helmut! Besides, it's forbidden at school."

"Well, they forbid a lot of things, and they can keep on forbidding them."

So authority is undermined here just like everywhere else. In the end, nothing at all is left. Now Jürgen, his face beaming, approaches Helmut and carefully turns his lapel over too; his face is transfigured. With a Mussolini-like gesture he lifts his arm to the ceiling and intones only "Heil! Helmut!"

At this very moment, a chorus rises from the street, "Helmut, you Nazi dumbass, aren't you coming down today?"

The brothers and sisters can only gawk at each other. Oddly enough, the first to open his mouth — and as one would expect, in a great rage — is Jürgen. But he passes up his rightful chance to forbid such foul-mouthed slander. Instead he turns to Helmut:

"It looks like you have a reputation as a hooligan. I'm not impressed by this kind of enthusiasm for the Party!"

"And I'm not impressed by people like you. It doesn't hurt us at all to be martyred by insults. It just makes us stronger."

49

But this is too much for Max. "Helmut, even if the school can't stop you from this kind of thing, we can. None of us are about to listen to this kind of talk from the youngest of us, still so immature and inexperienced. We're not going to talk about your party membership, because it wouldn't help anything to take away your swastika. We couldn't stop you from getting a new one anyway, and we can't shut you up in a glass cabinet either. We know you're going to do what you want. But there is one thing you should know: the rest of us are people too, with a will that is at least as good as that of you and your comrades. Those people outside called you a Nazi ass, and then you people call us dogs and fat cats. Neither side is right. Got that? Neither side. Where's it going to get us if we call each other murderers and dogs? Or if each ignores the exhausting work that the other does. Long ago we were known as a chivalrous people. Now our respect for our opponents has sunk as low as our cultural level. You treated your sister brashly, and you've even insulted your brother, one of your party comrades. And you think you're politically mature? Go to bed and think about how you can find a respectful basis for interaction with your brothers and sisters."

"But she hit me!"

"That was rash too, but maybe it's because she loves you."

Something in his brother's tone shocked Helmut. To hide his tears, he hurried out of the room, barely choking out a "Good night."

"Children," says Susie," I know I shouldn't have hit him. But I was so mad, because just today his teacher told me it would take a miracle to stop him from flunking again. Father doesn't care about anything anymore. I think the best thing we can do is pull him out of school."

"But then what? He'll just hang out on the corner with those other goons. Social Services says only 8% aren't involved in some kind of street crime."

Now Klara weighed in. "We shouldn't have been so hard on him, and shouldn't ask him to be such an exception, either. All of them today are politicized."

"That's because parents are too tired to look after their kids."

"Or because children won't listen to them."

"Politicized. All of them. That's bad. Things would be a lot quieter in this country if only the people who understand something about politics got involved. Just like women tend to vote the way their husbands, brothers, and boyfriends do, now children are becoming patsies as well. Then, when these patsies get the party bosses to where they want to be, the laws will be changed. You can count on it."

"But even with your pedagogy, Susi you won't be able to stop it."

"Come on. Think about it. Father spanked me, and all the rest of you too, except Jürgen, when he thought that he had to. We've turned out to be tolerably misbehaving children. Today we have sophisticated pedagogical theories, but children don't seem to be any better behaved, or more polite, or more gracious, or more free than we were. Don't you see just the opposite happening? Not only is their behavior worse, they have all sorts of complexes, too. Remember Moses, our old friend? He was enjoyed being subjected to all sorts of new ideas about child rearing while we were brought up the old-fashioned way. He never got the lightest boxing on the ears, and now do you see how unbearably arrogant he is, and yet highly needy. One wishes he'd get all the spankings now that he didn't get as a boy."

"Unbelievable, the modern Susi is for corporal punishment. Send him to Templin Prison, Susi."

"Don't be silly! I don't mean that we should test our feelings of power on prisoners. I'm just thinking along the lines of what Father used to say. I won't have any shilly shallying, and you've been shilly shallying too long. I can't help it, but I just don't think that dogs or children are fully responsible. I'm not impressed by the so-called majesty of childhood. And you all know that children really like me and will confide all their little worries to me, too. You were always astonished by Susi's kindergarten, where months went by without any child getting clopped, until one or another would have a meltdown. I'm just sorry that the mothers don't have enough money anymore to send their little ones to a private kindergarten. That was a wonderful job for a woman."

Elsa ponders this: even though Susi seems to be committed to old-fashioned ways of bringing up children, she has tact. She mentions Moses, whom they played with when they were children, but she really means Jürgen. In the second half of his school years he went to schools that were supposed to toughen up their students through sport and other activities. Today he's a sissy with a crummy education.

Dawn finally broke as they all crept off to bed.

Peter invited Elsa to stay with them rather than wander off to her house. Sitting beside her, he suddenly said, "You know what? I'll never understand you women. What happened tonight with Susi was completely unexpected. I just want to know one thing. Are you all happy these days, with your new cameraderie, equal rights, job opportunities, and free sexuality?"

"No Peter. We aren't." She paused, and then added, "Maybe it's because we've gone from one extreme to the other. What was supposed to be an attempt at harmony has become a pretty crummy bachelorhood."

Time flies by in this way, even as the catastrophe persists. Nobody knows what will come tomorrow: "Will I have a job?" "Will I have a meal to eat?"

All hope for a better future, if only because things can't get worse. Some place their hopes in Geneva, others in Lausanne.[6]

Gangs start street battles. City busses are ambushed. Gunfights break out in bars. It's hard to know who's the attacker, especially because provocation is also a kind of attack. Courtrooms are fuller than ever. Tumult rises to ever greater heights.

Each and every German family trembles. It has to be said that politics makes every German anxious. It's not only the politics, mind you; it's the not knowing where it's going to end. Life is almost in a state of suspended animation. No, this isn't life; it's a kind of nervous vegetating. Customs barriers are raised ever higher as foreign trade slows. The only trade that shows any signs of life is with Russia, and that's because of the Piatakov Treaty.[7] Even this doesn't help workers. No cash flows in, so nobody can be paid. The English pound has crashed. America has the bonus army and uncounted unemployed to deal with.[8] Even the dollar seems unsound. The world trembles, and the fault line runs through each and every family.

[6] The Geneva Conference of 1932–33, was meant to negotiate international dasarmament. The Lausanne Conference, also of 1932, which will fully occupy chapter 11, fixed a final total amount for German reparations for the First World War.

[7] In 1925 Germany and the Soviet Union signed an agreement to increase industrial trade that, in its attention to detail, became the model for other trade agreements between the USSR and the industrialized west.

[8] The bonus army was a collection of unemployed veterans of the First World War who marched on Washington, DC to demand the early payment of federal benefits which were not due for more than a decade.

CHAPTER FIVE

PARENTS SINK, AND LITTLE CHILDREN HAVE BIG WORRIES

POOR SUFFERING ELSA; she's barely able to keep going. The cursed need to be young is wearing her down. Nobody wants to acknowledge this, but it's true. Ironically, everybody seems to be aging even faster. She tries to stay young with the various drugs and concoctions of the day, everything that's advertised in the newspaper. In other words, if it shows up in a circular, she'll try it. She takes hormones, does exercises, even sits under a sunlamp. For days she seems to be refreshed. Indeed, she has succeeded in looking terrific, even though she's working more than twelve hours a day. But if she can't steal time for exercise and sun lamps she is tired to death.

And now she has to deal with this again. She once thought that she had a job for life. Because of this career position and the satisfaction it provides — even though she has to work hard — she has refused several offers of marriage. And now? Certainly she can make it a while longer. There's more to life than work. But a factory that had existed for more than a century with thousands of workers is being liquidated.

The liquidation brings with it an inhuman amount of work. Her bosses won't pay her any more to do it, but expect it as a kind of last gift from her. Obviously she isn't the *spiritus rector* of the negotiations, but she is responsible for grasping the ideas of twenty or more parties, recording them, taking dictation on all of the outstanding correspondence — sometimes even writing it herself! — making telephone calls, keeping the books, taking delivery of reports, and always being ready to stop everything should one of the company's directors call for her. And these days they call a lot.

In addition to everything else, they're trying to sell the factory complex, which is huge. This means negotiations with city departments, even with churches. Somebody thinks it would be a good idea, eventually, to build a hospital complex on the factory site. This is a quick deal breaker for the city authorities, who are already closing their existing hospitals despite the need for them, in order to save money. The churches want to build a special hospital. They think that this beautiful green strip on the city's edge is perfect for people recovering from venereal diseases. But this project too falls through after endless effort, because the people who live here set themselves against it: such a facility doesn't represent their vision of the neighborhood's character. Then a major film company steps forward, interested in the site. But unfortunately, as the negotiations progress their stock drops, and they don't have the money for such a multi-million-mark project. Then a foreign consortium has an interest. They want to build a new neighborhood on the plot. But the city administration doesn't want the foreign influence.

Finally, after all the endless efforts, there is no choice but for the government to give the old firm, which has brought Germany fame throughout the world, a subvention so that it can pay its workers their last checks and quietly wrap up its business. Then all lies fallow.

Elsa lives all of this with every fiber of her being. This is in addition to the upheaval in her country and her worry for her family.

Peter shines the only light at the end of the tunnel. He has a reasonable hope of landing a job as a foodstuffs chemist with a firm in England. This would be fantastic, as Peter could pick up the slack and help now when she, Elsa, can't anymore. When she is finished.

Even this hope, though, proves illusionary. The English firm sends a letter to express its great sorrow that it shan't be able to hire Peter Deutsch, whose dissertation is so very promising. It can't find a way around the Aliens Act, which allows one to volunteer in England for up to six months, but forbids employment.

Now Elsa can add Peter to her worries. He just sits there, doing nothing, as if something is about to happen. At the very least he could pound his fist on the table, but even that's too much. He sits as if he'll go crazy, or go out and hang himself. But just at this moment, he smiles at Susi and asks, "Susi, are you still going to your Russian hair stylist and your Hungarian tailor?"

Susi, though, is smart, and sees what he really wants to know. "Nope, little Peter. If England won't have you, I won't be helping out the foreign invasion here. I may not be an outspoken proponent of autarchy, but no more beautiful curls from the Russian and no more cheap and lovely dresses from the Hungarian, either. They were so polite, too. Oh well, 'Revanche pour Sadowa!'[1] This is so crazy. Inevitably one thing leads to another."

Brother Peter smiles, sitting so pale and used up, looking as if he wants to excuse himself for breathing. He can't afford books. He's cancelled the newspaper subscription. Still, he reads every scrap that his siblings bring into the house, or stands reading at the magazine kiosks.

---

[1] The Battle of Sadova (also known as the Battle of Königgrätz) was the bloodiest battle of the Austro-Prussian War of 1866, the war in which Prussia expelled Austria from German politics. Even though France was a neutral observer, "Revenge for Sadowa" became a popular slogan in France among those who thought that Prussia should be put in its place.

Elsa is left wishing that he at least had a serious girlfriend. Years ago Peter was as good as married. But after several years, his betrothed gave him his walking papers. She couldn't keep waiting for him to get a job, and the joy just bled out of their time together. Peter is nothing for the woman of today; he is too square.

Poor Elsa is now even more troubled.

She is less worried about Max. The boy is lively as spring. He's always busy, certainly going places more than staying home. It doesn't hurt that he has a sense of humor. For example, Max thinks that the brothers should form a collective for the purpose of finding a common activity for the unemployed members of the Deutsch family.

Even Jürgen is interested in this, and says in a friendly way: "Max, you're right. No more sitting around and waiting for me. It'll drive you nuts. If we could just find enough work to get a meal, a place to sleep, a suit, and a little pocket money. All of my friends think that would be just terrific."

"Are any of your friends workers, Jürgen?"

"Sure. Some even had good jobs."

"And?"

"What do you mean, 'and'?"

"Well, I mean, haven't they fought long and hard to get a decent wage for their work? How can they stand working for almost no money?"

"It's better than going crazy from waiting and hunger."

"So, they'd be happy to have mandatory work service? The same old militarism with a lighter touch."

"Do you really want to fight with me again? You can't forget that there's a moral side to this collapse. Nobody holds to the tariffs anymore. When things get better, wages will go up, too."

"I hope you're right. I'm just not sure that wages will adjust so soon to good times as quickly as they did to the bad times, and they'd have gone down even further if they hadn't been stopped. You will then need the people who put the brakes on the fall of wages, to start the climb back up. Or maybe you'll stay crouching on the path that you all thought was the only moral way out, and might still it think is."

"The one doesn't rule out the other. You mustn't think I'm asocial. I just think that unemployment benefits shouldn't be paid without some requirement of service in return. The Reich would be in better shape, and the unemployed would feel better about it, too. Why do you think that so many people are turning to Hitler? He knows how to put people to work, how to give them things to do. This alone makes him a genius. He has grasped psychologically what we are lacking at this point in time."

"There's a lot of truth in what you say, Jürgen. But Hitler is promising better times, and he won't be able to deliver. To help some, he's going to have to hurt others. And if he wanted to free his regiments from the night-mare of inactivity, he could let them really work, not just exercise."

"But Max, there's no work to give them"

"Jürgen, now you're contradicting yourself. First you give a well-thought-out plea for the mandatory work requirement, then you admit the truth: there's no work, or at least no way to pay for work. In other words, the way things stand now there's no work in trade because there's no money. Hitler's had lots of money available, and if he had used it to create work, he'd have won a whole world, not just built a huge political party. Who could have stopped the leader of such a big, private party, which until recently it still was, from building bridges, streets, train lines, dams, and so on? The Baltic is always stealing land from us. What a deed it would it have been if Hitler had helped connect the Hallig Islands and Borkum to the mainland. Work, land to settle, all of it could have been done. But instead — and you're right here, he is quite the psychologist — he decided to work with racial hatred and militarism. Once, when I was a boy, I told Peter that Germans are happy to be soldiers, and now, do you see, Hitler grasps that, too?

The only thing is that racism is going to rub too many people the wrong way, because the Germans are no longer just blond, heroic-aryan giants with racially pure blood. Unfortunately, most are average sized and round. But things like that make for good propaganda, and people who don't fit the bill wish that they did."

Elsa's not afraid of a fighting cock like Max. He amuses her, probably because they're two of a kind.

"Better a sharp tongue than a knife in your pocket," says Max.

"Max, what do you do with all your time?"

"Elsa, I know you won't believe it, but I don't have enough time to do what I want." Thus says Max, who always has some pocket money. Elsa has a hunch that this Ph.D. in economics walks around, hat tipped back on his head, hands stuffed into his pockets, whistling a tune, or doing stupid temporary jobs.

Max ambles along the streets and chats up every girl who catches his fancy. He links arms with them and, standing before the colorful displays at KaDeWe,[2] gives them advice about which clothes they should wear. They talk about sports, then about Schopenhauer. In the end he decides that she's just a silly goose. What a waste of time. No wonder the girls can't under-

---

[2] KaDeWe, or Kaufhaus des Westens, was, and still is, Europe's largest department store, with a selection of goods ranging from high fashion to gourmet foods from around the world. During the Weimar Republic it had Jewish ownership, but after 1933 the Nazis mandated that the store be "Aryanized."

stand him: when they chirp, "oh what a nice car?" Max answers laconically, "But it only runs on electricity." Or he might walk with them on a quiet, villa-lined street, and they say, "umm, life must be good in one of those mansions!" and he responds, "I'll bet that next week a red auction bill will be posted on one of those trees out front." Max might sometimes add, "The soles of my shoes may have holes in them, but they're at least paid for. His tires aren't." Really, what girl would get any of this?

Max sees what he sees, and knows the score. Nothing can take him in.

Just once, though, as he is about to jog across Potsdamer Strasse, even as he stands considering whether he should go to the Institute for Politics or perhaps to the Wertheim Department store — just to see what kind of swim-suit this year's fashionable girl is wearing — both his heart and his head freeze. He's standing at the corner of Luetzow Strasse when he sees four stormtroopers, whom he'd half noticed a moment earlier, eyeing a slight girl in a very obvious way.

Aha, he thinks, four guys checking out one girl. Good God, these boys really are desperate.

There isn't anything really special about the girl. She's not really pretty. She's not even made up. Just one of the thousands of tired girls who leave their offices behind around this hour and start their private lives.

Wait a second? The small woman shrinks back oddly against the side of the building, crowded by the thugs.

"Hmmm. Let's just stay here for a minute and see what develops."

The development doesn't take too long. One of the goons grabs the girl by the arm while she tries to pull away. Her hat flies. And then she takes a kick in the stomach from another one of the four and slumps down.

"What, he kicked her!" Max screams, and springs in great strides across the avenue, even though the traffic light turns green and cars start moving. He gets there just in time to save her from further blows. Jumping on the "boys" from behind, he pulls one back, hits the second one in the neck, and throws a few well-placed punches. One of the four pulls a whistle out of his pocket, and is about to call more of his comrades to action, but Max is just able to pull it out of his hand in time. Although a crowd begins to collect and passively encircles the combatants, and one hears things said like how unheard of and how coarse it is to kick a woman in the stomach, Max no-tices that nobody steps in to help him. If he doesn't disappear fast, he won't be able to hold out against them, since the attackers are sure to get re-inforcements. He doles out a few more punches to the chin, as body blows won't do it for him this time. These 18-year-olds are weak. Max picks the girl up off of the pavement like a helpless bundle that doesn't understand what's going on. Angry, his collar torn, his jacket dirtied, his brown hair in his eyes, Max yells, "Out of my way. What's the matter with you? Grab us a cab, quick!"

People do make room for him, though only reluctantly, because the show is over. A taxi driver calls out, "hurry up, young man." Max sets the young woman down in the cab and throws himself down on the seat beside her. Then the cab peels out, breaking all traffic laws.

High time, too. A storm is breaking out on the street. Max can't see it, but communists are assembling on the other side of the avenue. "These 'heroes' have kicked a girl in the stomach. Is this what all of you want to see?"

"But she's a Jewish girl!"

"Big deal! A woman's a woman."

Thus begins yet another street rumble.

As they pull away, the driver turns his head and asks Max where he wants to go. "Man, let's go to the emergency room," says Max, wiping his sweaty hair back, "maybe we can get a cognac. This poor girl's still passed out."

She starts to come to in the ER, but not until Max has had another confrontation. "Are you the young lady's brother? Maybe you're the fiancé? What is her name?. . . ." and so on. Max, still worked up, gets rude; saying that if they keep asking questions, she might just come to by herself. "We're strangers. All I know is that somebody kicked her in the stomach."

Carefully he and the driver put the girl back into the taxi. As he sizes up the driver, he asks, "Will you take us a little farther? I can't pay the fare."

"Don't worry about it. Just get in," says Max's new friend.

"How can I thank you?" whispers the girl. "Don't worry about it" says Max, once again full of superiority. "Just tell me where you live and we'll know where to take you."

She gives her address.

"God!" cries Max, throwing a comical look to the driver. "The girl lives all the way out in Steglitz?"[3]

Something about the man's heaving back shows Max that his new friend is laughing. With this, Max laughs, too. For the first time today, maybe for the first time in a month, and it is such a freeing feeling. He's rescued somebody. Even in the pale face of the girl there rises a quiet smile.

"Whaddya know?," thinks Max, "She has pretty eyes — gray blue. On the whole, she's cute. There's even something exotic about her dark hair and bright eyes . . . a complexion like ivory." Max is on the point of shrink-

---

[3] A largely middle-class suburb in Berlin's southwest. When most people thought of Steglitz, they imagined the very upscale neighborhoods. Like most of the city's districts, though, it also had its poorer corners.

ing reservedly into the corner. He looks for his brashness, but can't find it anywhere.

Max's friend drives down Hauptstrasse until it seems to become tired of its name and changes it first into Rheinstrasse and then Schlossstrasse. It's a splendid street, full of shops, movie theaters, and government buildings. Then the friend turns into a side street, and the shine disappears as fast as the sun sets in the tropics. Old houses, mended clothing hanging on lines, sad gardens all greet the eye. The car stutters over a temporary bridge ringed by broken plaster and latticed fences. Wedged between the ornate, old buildings are two newer buildings. It almost looks as if an artist had shone a false light onto his canvas. Incredibly incongruous, but so symbolic. Two eras, side-by-side. Almost as if the houses are ready to attack each other, especially the new, aggressive ones. The old ones stand in a reflective, almost sleepy way as if to say, "We have solid foundations, even if our plaster is a bit cracked. Our walls are strong. We have survived the fates without cheating our tenants. Our walls have held both sorrow and joy. You should be like us."

Max asks his charge her name.

"Maria."

"So, Maria? Don't you have a last name?"

"Of course. It's Sommer."

"Hmmm. That's a nice, warm name. There . . ."

The car jerks to a stop, interrupting Max. The two men help Maria Sommer climb out, and she asks them if they will walk her up to her family's apartment.

The chauffeur, though, doesn't want to leave the car alone. "The times are so uncertain," he says.

"I would like to offer you something to drink and pay for the ride, but I don't have any money on me," says Maria.

"Then you can send it to me when you get the chance, little miss. I'd have driven you for free, though, in such a bad situation."

Maria shakes his hand warmly, takes down his address, and promises to send the money today.

"Yeah, yeah. It's OK. You won't run away." The big man shuffles and looks embarrassed. "I just wanted to say that you really should know that we're not all so bad. Now, don't forget to go to a doctor soon, just to be sure that you're really alright."

Max is up and running again. Only with great difficulty is he able to stop himself from making a cheeky remark about things turning out all right. Instead, he just grins and tells the driver that he, Max, would be very happy if his newfound friend would come by for a visit. With a "Done," the two part ways.

59

"Now come with me, you poor thing. You've stood long enough," he says, gently leading Maria.

Upstairs, Maria unlocks the door quietly and leads him quickly into a kind of hybrid kitchen/living room.

But first she wants to tell her parents half the truth, so as not to scare them too much, she says.

There sits Max in the middle of a strange house, barely different from the middle-class house of his own parents. The biggest difference is that the silver candlesticks have another shape than those that the family Deutsch used for celebrations — before they went to the pawn shop. The carpet is exactly as worn and the buffet is just as old fashioned as the one in his house. Now and again he hears Maria's deep voice coming through the door as she talks with her parents.

As he studies the copperplate etching of "Potsdamerplatz 100 Years Ago" and throws a sidelong glance at an open book, Maria comes in with her parents.

It occurs to Max that he will soon have to introduce himself, and yet he has the impression that all the good manners he's been taught would be out of place. He smiles when he thinks about the impression he would make if he clicked his heels together smartly like his brother Jürgen did when he was officially introduced, adding his name by way of a totally superfluous bark. Instead he says quietly, as is his usual style:

"Pardon me, please, for showing up with a torn collar. I'm Max Deutsch. I don't want to keep you, as I see that your daughter is back in good hands."

Herr Sommer, a small, thin man who appears somewhat sickly, steps toward Max, taking his hand in both of his own, and says, "Please, Herr Deutsch, won't you stay for a little while? Our daughter told us what you did for her, and that she probably wouldn't be here if it weren't for you."

Maria's mother breaks in with a desperate look: "Herr Deutsch, we . . ." but can't get any farther, because tears are choking her voice off.

Max isn't quite ready for any of this. He stands there, almost crumpling into himself, and stutters, "Ma'am, please, everything is fine now. And Herr Sommer, please don't thank me. It was the only thing to do. I'm just embarrassed that something like this could happen."

"Just one question, Herr Deutsch," Herr Sommer whispers. "Are you a Christian?"

"Yes, but if that was an example of Christianity, then I may just quit."

"Oh, the God of all religions is the same, even if his names change."

"Do you really believe that, Herr Sommer? Even when we see how the religions fight against each other every day? I'm Protestant, but like lots of others I never go to church. They never did know how to hold onto me. But why did you ask if I'm a Christian?"

60

"Because I want to know, along with my wife, that a Christian made good what another Christian did."

"I have to say that you are able to forgive more quickly than I. And it's my God who teaches, 'He giveth his cheek to him that smiteth him . . .' No, no. Even that's not right. I just don't have any intention of letting my fellow Christians knock my teeth out."

While this is going on, Maria calms her mother down and starts up a very old-fashioned coffeemaker. A soft singing sound wafts through the room while the aroma of spirits catches the nose and gives the pleasure of anticipation. Max decides that this was a great idea, even though Maria should probably going to sleep in her little bed instead. All of his thoughts about Maria take diminutive form, because she strikes him as such a cute little thing.

Old plates and delicate cups with fine etching are put on the table. Maria's mother explains that her ancestors were forced by the "Old Fritz" to buy them in great quantities from the Royal Porcelain Works to get permission to marry.[4]

Max quickly mentions that he has such a gluttonous appetite that he should leave so that the Sommers won't think that he's impolite. But they keep him there, and Max enjoys one of the nicest family evenings that he's had in years. He finds out that Herr Sommer has just lost his job as a buyer, a job that he's held for years, because embroidered cloth from Switzerland has been replaced by more fashionable material. He learns that Maria was going to study singing, had even started, but now works in an office. A picture, beneath which, on a small shelf, there are candles and flowers, is taken down from its place on the wall and passed around. That's how he meets Leo, their son. Written on it, in a shaky hand and partially smeared from tears, is the line "Fallen on the Field of Honor, 1917."

Max's hand shakes. He can't say what he's thinking, but everyone knows anyway — that there sits an honorable man — and comes to the conclusion that even though Jews did right, afterward people said that they had shirked.

Mother has tears in her eyes again. Maria stands up, goes to the piano and sings a wonderful, strange song. Her voice is clear, dark, and soft. The very masculine Max is almost in tears. He thinks about how torn his own family is, and the harmony that he finds here despite all the sorrow.

"My only child," says Herr Sommer, looking across the table — and Maria sings.

---

[4] The "Old Fritz" was Frederick II (the Great), Prussian monarch from 1740 to 1786. Frederick is generally credited with putting Prussia on the road to great power status by a series of military victories which greatly enlarged Prussian territory.

Max thinks about how he used to sing, but no tone comes into his throat now, and the songs that he knows are so old. Still, he would love to sing with the girl.

As it gets late, he leaves the Sommers. They ask him to come back, but Max has another request, one that lays heavy on his heart. Finally, though, he says that he would like to check in on Maria again, to see how she is getting on. Just to be sure that she gets home safely from her office, he offers to walk her home tomorrow.

Despite everything, Max is in a great mood today. In fact, he would run all the way home if he could. For one thing, he really wants to chat with Elsa about his experience. Hopefully she'll be at the house. She's always having to work so late these days; something just isn't right.

When he arrives home, his brothers and sisters are in state fit to be tied. At first he can't even begin to understand what's going on. Finally he understands: they have heard on the radio that the president has dismissed the tough old chancellor.[5] So much for the quiet times; they're gone. Max is horrified. "Again? This is like a revolving door!"

Baffled, he asks, "Did he slave away so hard in vain, didn't he prevent civil war until now, even if he did employ harsh measures? Will a new chancellor be able to govern without emergency decrees? Haven't the chancellor's emergency measures made as many people happy as they've scared? Isn't he the only one who was able to get rents and prices to drop like wages have — even if not far enough? Isn't he the first one who said 'no' to foreign governments? 'Economize, economize.' That made him some enemies. So, we're going to break everything off? Try something new? We must be cursed! Now what's going to happen?"

Peter says: "Even if he and his cabinet are leaving office now, I don't think that his career's over."

Jürgen, though, is triumphant: "Now it's the Führer's turn."

Susi screams at him: "If he would actually do something, your Führer. I won't be the last one to say something good about him if he can really improve things. He's already given up his show of nonchalance in regard to other countries. Maybe he really can do something. But he should finally prove it."

[5] President Paul von Hindenburg dismissed Chancellor Heinrich Brüning from office in May, 1932. Some historians view Brüning as the last democratically minded chancellor of the republic, others as the first in a series of antidemocratic chancellors which ultimately led to the appointment of Adolf Hitler in January, 1933. Either way, Brüning was the first chancellor to rely on the president's use of emergency powers to govern in the face of an unsympathetic parliament.

Even Helmut has to agree with this. "In our Jungsturm everybody says that if he doesn't do what he promises, we'll be the harshest judges."[6]

Elsa calls the siblings together for a family meeting. The parents have to attend too. Pitt Deutsch sits with his shellac samples as usual, while Mother lies in bed. "Does it have to be today, Elsa?"

"Yes," Elsa answers harshly, "it does."

She tells the family that her job is set to disappear in three months. She does have a small bank account, and it should be enough to hold the family above water — in the manner in which they've been living — for about six months from her job's end. That means nine more months of security, however meager. What will come after that, she doesn't know yet. Under these circumstances she holds it to be out of the question for Helmut to stay in school, especially because he's just flunked another grade.

Mother moans. Pitt Deutsch muddles his shellac samples and beakers together. Otherwise, nothing.

The council of siblings decides to pull Helmut from school and find him a job — even the most menial will do.

Helmut's annoyance shows. "You want me to be a delivery boy?!"

This wakes Pitt up. Slamming his hand on the table so that the beakers shake, he roars, "Yes. You will be a delivery boy, you lazy jerk! If your mother and father weren't too proud to drive a dogcart through the city — and the times were a lot better then — then the son can start out as a delivery boy and not lose face."

"I won't," he sobs defiantly.

The old Herr Deutsch gets up, leaning heavily on his cane, on which he often depends due to rheumatism, and walks threateningly towards his youngest son. His eyes well with tears. His hate for the entire age comes into his mind. He hits the boy in a way he never hit his other children. Peter and Max spring between them. Herr Pitt Deutsch, an old man, collapses, ashen-faced.

A little later Elsa takes Max aside to talk with him about Peter.

"I'm begging you, Max, to think of a way to keep Peter busy. It's not so important that he earn money, just that he stops sitting around thinking so much. It's like he's dying. Max, I'm not waiting for your great idea that's going to help all of us; just find something for Peter to do. You can see that his wheels are spinning, spinning so hard that he can't come up with anything for himself. For God's sake, come up with something soon, or I don't know what will happen to him!"

---

[6] The Jungsturm (Young Storm) was the youth division of the Nazi Stormtroopers (SA or Sturmabteilung).

63

Max, of course, promises to do his best. But about his own affair of to-day he says not a word more.

The siblings have taken Helmut out of school and after a lot of hard work have secured a delivery job for him at a small grocery. It's still possible, even today, to get some jobs if only you keep pressing.

Helmut earns twelve marks a week, and can get as much as three more in tips. Indeed, the first weeks go really well, but it isn't long before prob-lems start. The manager says that Helmut is obstinate. He knows everything better than anybody else, talks back constantly, and breaks eggs and beer bottles. These are deducted from his wages. The family has to intervene, as well, when he doesn't bring enough money back after he's finished his de-livery runs. It hurts the manager to say it, but if anything more goes wrong, he'll be let go. Naturally, this doesn't take long. One evening, shortly before 7:00, when he is supposed to make one more quick delivery nearby, Helmut says that he won't do it, as he wants to make it to the playing field on time.

"These are hard times," says the manager, coolly, "but it's your deci-sion. Either do what your job requires, and take the five minutes to do the delivery, or you're fired."

With the words, "Then I'm fired," Helmut walks out. As far as he's con-cerned, his mother can go by to pick up his paperwork. Now, Helmut too sits around the house. Because he's so young, he isn't entitled to any gov-ernmental support, and when he's home he's brazen and insulting.

On the other hand, he's seldom home. He won't tell anybody where he is, but his brothers and sisters think he's at a Party facility, playing cards, reading Party material, and doing Jungsturm exercises with his comrades. Sometimes, he's gone for as much as a week at a time. Those times, he's probably staying in a tent.

Herr Pitt Deutsch has sunk back into his funk, and Mother sneaks some pocket change to Helmut when he brusquely demands it from her.

The strange thing is that Jürgen doesn't look out for him. Even though they're in the same Party, they've become estranged.

Now Max, who picks up Maria every day, spends time at the Sommers' home from time to time, and still hasn't told his family about his adventures, has cares of his own. Maria's vacation is coming soon, and she wants to go somewhere in the countryside for some rest and relaxation. Although he hasn't pushed their relationship further, he knows that he'll really miss her.

On the other hand, he has an idea to keep Peter busy. It's the least that he can do for his poor, harried favorite sister. One day, he takes Peter aside to say, "You're a chemist, and certainly know the basics, even if you special-ize in foodstuffs. What do you think about this? What would happen if we took LACAID or something similar and coated thin metal disks with it to make cheap gramophone records? It's not as if we have anything better to do. What do you think? Should we give it a try?"

"Sure, but where will we get the material?"

"Father still has all the samples, and there's still LACAID in the basement. He just couldn't bear to get rid of it."

This starts to wake Peter up. "Hmmm! LACAID doesn't need to be heated to high temperatures. But where will we find a press?"

"Good point. You see, I didn't think about that. Is there some other heavy thing we could use? We might have something made of iron in the basement. First, of course, you would have to make mixtures. Maybe they could be made more inexpensively than LACAID. It doesn't have to be exactly LACAID. Only I don't understand enough about it. Maybe you could talk to Father about it a little too. After all, he knows a great deal about it. Come down into the basement with me, maybe we'll find something else that you could use." With this, Max has Peter's full attention.

He is able to light a balky old lantern, and they are on their way. Max doesn't think much of his own idea, but it was an excellent thought to get his father involved with it as well. Pleased, he goes with his brother into the cellar.

Soon they're schlepping heavy bags upstairs. Although they find one of the old wash-boilers, they don't see anything heavy that could be used to press materials together.

About the time he's wanting to pull his hair out in frustration, Max's glance lands in one of the basement's corners. There stands an old copy press. With two once-shiny ball bearings, now tarnished brown, a screw-down spindle running through its center, and two round plates on either side, it was once used to copy letters. Heaven knows why Pitt Deutsch ever saved such an old-fashioned thing. Surely even he couldn't have used it for very long.

"Hey Peter," Max called into the darkness, "do you need a hydraulic press for the damned LACAID?"

"No, I don't think it's hard to press."

Max then drags the press into the light.

"Look at what I've got here."

With astonishment, the two brothers inspect the thing from all sides. They soon discover an inscription on top, that, although smudged, would have been on it forever, or at least until it was scrapped. With patience they finally decipher the blackened bronze: "WITH GOD!"

A good introduction to the old accounting.

"All right!" says Max, "Peter, WITH GOD! it is."

CHAPTER SIX

POLITICS MAKES A SHOCKING ENCROACHMENT

T HE FATE OF THE FAMILY DEUTSCH was already sealed at the movies once. This was when Herr Deutsch saw a film, a form still in its infancy, and pondered what could become of an encircled "Fort Germany."

This next time, in front of his family, he flew into empty-headed forgetfulness.

Today, the entire family, except for Elsa and Helmut, have also decided to escape themselves by fleeing into the cinema. Susi was able to engineer this by means of some discount tickets she'd come across. Even though it's a third-run theater, the program is interesting, varied, and long — a bit of something for everybody. Herr Deutsch can feast on a film full of beer, potato salad, and parades, chock full of the delights of the military life.

Max, on the other hand, finds himself annoyed by a one-act short that's nothing but a poor variation of the brilliant Mickey Mouse. Italian airplane maneuvers and a parade of American warships are enough to stoke Jürgen's enthusiasm. Now it's time (finally! think Klara and Susi) for the feature film. Fair enough, it's not a first-run film. But it's so Hungarian, full of broken-hearted romance, beautiful cinematography, and sweet, almost bird-like singing. Well, Max isn't quite sure. He finds the peeping to be more like squeaking, and it gets on his nerves. To be frank, he's secretly annoyed that he cut short his evening with Maria to have to sit through such nonsense. For Klara, though, the voices are like Stradivarius's, while Susi is simply delighted by the diva's dresses and four-poster bed. It occurs to Jürgen that the star shouldn't be so silly as to sit in the bathtub and make a telephone call. Why, the silly cow could electrocute herself! Peter, playing the teacher, instructs his brother that the charge is too weak for that. He's only half paying attention, though. His concentration is on his first solution to the LACAID problem, and he's already developing a second to try tomorrow. Finally, Max looks over at Susi, wide-eyed and open-mouthed, and can't help but tease her. Finally, the people behind the family Deutsch can't take their yammering anymore: "SHUSH!"

The film draws to its not very exciting end — we all know how such movies end, don't we? — as a voice rings out across the theater: "Is there a Deutsch family here? You're needed immediately!"

The Deutsch family stares at one another in shock. Max tells the others to sit tight while he goes out and sees what the matter is.

As he reaches the foyer, bedecked with posters of soon-to-be forgotten film legends, Max sees Elsa, red faced and sitting slumped on a chair. He has to shake her before she even recognizes him. She jumps up and collapses on the chair again. Max simply doesn't recognize her as the superior sister he otherwise knows.

"What happened? What's the matter?"

"Huh? Oh yeah. Aren't Mother and Father inside? We have to go to the morgue right away."

Thinking that his sister has lost her mind, he grabs her firmly by the arm.

"Max. Listen to me. They shot our baby brother on the street. When I got home, I forgot that you all went to the movies. There were lot of people gathered in front of the house, and the woman who works in the dairy store came up to me with tears in her eyes:

"O God, Fräulein Deutsch, it's horrible. Go straight to the police. People were asking for all of you, but nobody was home."

"But Frau Khulmey, please tell me what happened."

"We don't know exactly. The kids were running down the street into the houses and screaming that Helmut Deutsch had been shot. Then the police came and searched all the houses. They arrested a couple of the kids, and picked up a pile of propaganda flyers off the street."

"I couldn't listen any more and went straight to the police station. They told me that the kids said that the dead boy was named Helmut Deutsch. They've already sent the body to the morgue. They said that our parents have to view the body to make a positive identification."

"Good God!" Max stammers. Even as Max's jaw drops open, the doors to the cinema open too, and hundreds of people pour out of the movie. Elsa and Max wait for their parents, brothers, and sisters to come out and then guide them to the street, hailing two taxis as they do.

Susi asks, "What's happening? Have you gone crazy?"

"No. Something terrible has happened. Mother, Father, please, get in." Max reports what he has heard as mercifully as possible. In her anxiety, the color drains out of Frau Deutsch's face.

"Maybe it's not him at all whom we're going to see, maybe he's still out in the tents with his comrades, and all this anxiety is for nothing," says Susi.

What a sorrowful ride. As the taxis turn off at the Oranienburger Gate, Pitt Deutsch begins to cry and blurts out, "And on top of everything else, I hit him! No one can do anything about that."

The children have to lead the parents, who are now at the point of total breakdown, into this horrible building, where the nameless whose luck has run out and the "impounded" lie. Their youngest son, though, isn't yet upstairs on ice; he still lies in the cellar.

Their feet don't want to descend the stairs. The air takes their breath away. A serious man, pulls the sheet back: "Do you recognize this young man as your son, Helmut Deutsch?"

Fate deals a hard blow. Mother collapses onto the floor, unconscious. Father sobs, "Yes, that's him." He tries to stroke his youngest's dirty cheeks with his old, gouty hands. The serious man turns back to him and says quietly and gently, "Please don't touch him." Still, he overlooks it, as Pitt continues to stroke his son. Klara and Susi can't stop crying. Only Peter, Elsa, and Max stare, dry-eyed into space, while Jürgen, chalk-white, paces back and forth nervously.

Frau Martha is carried back to the car, her face and throat a sickly blue, her breath almost a death rattle. Peter looks at her, and whispers, "I'm worried about Mother. We should take her to a hospital. This is horrible." Elsa and Max look and nod their heads as they sneak a sidelong look at their father. He is sitting apathetically, tears running, unchecked, down his face.

Standing around the hospital, the group waits for the doctor.

"Herr Doctor, What is it? Will she have to . . .?"

He shrugs his shoulders, "Herr Dr. Deutsch, of course we will do all that is medically possible. In three weeks or so we'll know whether she can survive this."

Her brothers and sisters have to wrestle Klara out, who wants to stay with her mother. Pitt Deutsch hurries out wearing a face that looks as if none of this has anything to do with him.

A mother lies, lonely, in a large building, cut off from all that had once surrounded her. Alone and surrounded by strangers, she follows her youngest in death.

CHAPTER SEVEN

THE ONE MOST ABLE TO SURVIVE PULLS NEW HOPE OUT OF CHAOS

M AX RUNS AROUND IN HIS GRAY SUIT, a black band tied on the sleeve. Even proper mourning is impossible in these days. All the children are broke, and it makes no sense for Elsa to spend her last money on this. Did Helmut want to die for his beliefs? Did Mother love them all as much as she did him? Such brooding makes one sick. Maybe if he could have found an upright, sensible, adult Party man to speak with, maybe it all would have made some sense. Maybe he could have learned something reasonable.

With their bravura and their threatening drivel, the very young — who aren't even old enough to vote, but still are convinced by the unscientific and spiteful articles of a few newspapers and the certainly dazzling and impressively spoken words of certain orators, none of which would convince a thinking person — ah, these easily controllable youth get such an incomplete picture of the world. What was it that Jürgen said? "We're sometimes not so far apart in how we see the world"? What is right and what is wrong? What's coming next? Peter thinks "War and civil war." Elsa says, "Compromise and a new socialist impulse, because the ones have been fighting with methods that they will later regret having used." Jürgen's view is: "Now everything will be fine: a man of strong will is going to act on your behalf and teach you how to think of yourselves. Only when foreigners once again fear us will they again treat us with respect. They won't be proud and armed to the teeth while we have not a soldier to be seen. The arrogance of the others will subside, and for that you will have our Führer to thank."

"Jürgen," Susi answers, "The president has sent the Reichstag home because it doesn't represent the majority of the people anymore. Now he's brought back the kind of people that Father has always admired. Do you really think that this is what most people want? Right now you're the biggest party, even though you don't have a majority, but you're a *socialist workers* Party and your chief is a man from the people. Why haven't National Social- ist workers taken over the Reichstag? I just don't get it. The Reichstag has been sent packing because it doesn't represent the majority of the popula- tion, and the new government is cobbled together out of leaders of very small parties — even if, apart from the context, they may be of good will. You and your comrades are claiming joyfully that your Führer is about to take over. True enough, he has the biggest party behind him. Please tell me why we got a cabinet of barons instead? I don't want an opinion, just an explanation of the contradictions that no German can understand."

Ever since his brother's death — and his mother's death that followed — Jürgen has become both quieter and more contemplative. His answer to Susi is so much quieter than anything anybody's heard from him in a long time:

"Susi, I don't understand it either, but I really think that the election is going to clear everything up. There's so much that I don't get anymore. Our party has sacrificed so many members; it just can't be for nothing. They only wanted what was best."

"The best," interjected Max, "is what everybody else wanted for their Fatherland too. But what is to be seen as best is relative. One wants the best for the people who live in the country. Another wants the best for the country itself. But let's wait and see what happens; we've seen too much, experienced too much to get so worked up now. We can be sure of two things; that tomorrow won't be perfect, and that we've still got a long way to go before we get over the war."

It's better with Maria, thinks Max. There he hardly talks about politics. They don't talk about the attack that brought them together, either. For Max, Maria is the one constant in a crazy world. Only once did she lose her calm and gentleness and launch into a passionate excoriation of the craziness of the day. That was not long before, when she saw how broken up Max was about the deaths of his brother and mother, when, in a disturbed state, he came to visit, tried to put his feelings into words, couldn't, and simply buried his head in his arms on the kitchen table and cried bitter tears.

"Do you see!" she cried, to nobody in particular, "how presumptuous it is to think that we're the only ones who are hunted down?!"

After they both had taken a few days to calm back down, they decided to go on an afternoon walk through the Steglitz City Park. After a long rain all the greenery looks so freshly washed. Looking through the trees they could see white-clad figures chasing after tennis balls on clean, well-demarcated courts.

"Please God, just let us avoid politics!" thinks Max as he points out to Maria all of the park's sights. "Maria, look at the American Birch trees, the way that they always grow in pairs. They don't seem to have any trouble finding each other. By the way, when are you going to desert us?"

"I think in about eight days."

"Well that's all I needed."

Maria scrunched one eye closed — only because of the sun, of course — and, thus blinded, looked up at Max, who towered above her by at least a head.

"Tell me, Max, do you think that a relatively frugal person could get by on three marks fifty a day?"

"Of course. Why do you need to go to the spa? Take a vacation in the countryside if you really want to get away. That way, too, you'll certainly be able to spend less."

Maria smiled up at him. "I shouldn't try to meet people, should I, Max?"

"As far as I'm concerned, you should meet as many people as you like, if that's fun for you. Hopefully you won't be so tied up that you forget to send me a little postcard, though."

Max is being cheeky, to put it directly. He's also feeling very uneasy. Not to see Maria for ten days? He'll have to start strolling the streets again, or convince Peter to try a new mixture, as the others simply won't stick to metal. And now, on top of everything, to imagine Maria among the kind of people who can afford a vacation. And on top of that the girl is acting like an imp today and looks so happy about her plans to go away so soon.

Max would like to tell her what he's really thinking, but thinks, do I have the right to? After all, doesn't she really need a vacation after a year of hard work? Even the unemployed sit outside by the water and sun themselves, and here he, in his egoism, is supposed to spoil her vacation? Dear God, if only he had a few cents to rub together! He knows what he'd suggest then.

"What's the matter, Max? Cat got your tongue?"

"It's nothing. I was just thinking."

"So was I, Max."

"If it's not a secret, then you can tell me."

"Gladly. Hopefully, you'll share your dark thoughts with me, too, the ones that are so easy to read on your face, I mean. In short, I thought that the seven marks per day — not counting train fare — that I've saved is far too much for me, since I've already decided not to visit the high-end resorts. And then I thought that you once told me how your sister Elsa said "And Germany itself is so beautiful." You told me then how compellingly she said it. And I — — and we — — Max, I don't know how to say this. I only mean that we could both stand to get out into nature, but I don't know where I should go, and I thought that maybe you'd have some of your sister's enthusiasm and could show me Germany.

Max, don't make me talk so much. You know what I'm suggesting. I think it would be so nice to travel with you. Max, would you like to? There's enough money for us both."

"If you went with me, Maria, we'd have to walk, not ride. But, how could you think such a thing? I can't let you pay my way! That would just be wrong."

73

"I don't understand you! One day when you earn some money, you can pay my way."

They argue over the possibility or impossibility of it. Finally, after about an hour, Max remarked that as far as he was concerned, it could get a bit darker in the park.

"What does that have to do with our trip?" asked Maria, astonished.

"Not much, really," purred Max, delightedly, "I just wanted to give a salty kiss to a splendid girl."

Maria's laugh rung like a bell. "You're such a youngster, to make an offer first before you give a girl a kiss."

New worries occurred to Max. "And what would your parents say, Maria?"

"Oh, they already know. Mother thinks it's quite indecent. She's trying, though, to understand the times. She asks these silly questions, like, 'will you stay in separate rooms?' and so on. Parents always think that something will happen if they're not around. As if something couldn't happen in their own house that they wouldn't like. But I don't like keeping secrets from my parents. It might be simpler just to lie to them. But I think that would be the weak, cowardly side of modern youth. Everybody knows what's going on, but rather than be open about it, they hide it. Just like in the old days. Father is more modern. He says, 'Stop, Mama. We can trust the Deutsch boy with our girl.'

So you see, they have a good opinion of you. Don't start feeling too good about yourself, though."

With this, Max practically jumps for joy. Maria responds by digging her elbow into his ribs. But she spares him the details of her parents' reaction. They had a lot more against her inviting Max, and her father's speech was somewhat longer, too.

What he really said was: "mama, listen to me. I don't believe that Deutsch will make our daughter unhappy. Besides, he couldn't ask for Maria's hand, even if he wanted to. Why would he? He can't even feed himself, how could he go courting?"

"Yes but what will come of all this? Maria says that she's in love with Max Deutsch and he seems to be in love with her, too. Now she wants him to travel with her, and we're supposed to just sit back and watch? There is just no way!"

"Yes mama," said the quiet, small Herr Sommer, "A few years ago, I wouldn't have permitted it either. If she's in love with him — and she wouldn't love a bad man — but he can't marry her because he's unemployed, and we can't give her a dowry anymore, either, she can't be expected to renounce all the joys of life. She's also not young enough anymore to put all her hopes on hold. We just have to let young people today get whatever happiness they can out of their terrible lives. That's not cultural Bolshevism by a long shot."[1]

Maria doesn't want to add any moral burden to Max's already heavy load, so she withholds her parents' further remarks. Instead, they begin to make plans. While Maria is quietly happy, Max could jump out of his skin.

"First, you have to meet Elsa. This is non-negotiable." Elsa's blessing, you see, means a great deal to Max. In fact, he's going to speak with her tonight. With this decided, he starts to lay out his travel plans. First idea — Southern Germany. On the one hand, the people there are quite stubborn. On the other, they're incredibly nice. But, they do hate Prussians. "You know, Maria, that's because they get so bossed around by Berlin. But they have nothing against us as individuals. They're like my brother, Jürgen, always surprised that we often think the same way as them. Such nice folks, and what a beautiful accent, too." Unfortunately, train fare to South Germany is too high, and it's back to the drawing board. Next he wants to go with her to Pomerania. "Usedom has a lovely coast, a coast with not a single pebble and beautiful snow white sand. You could brush your teeth with it. Woods behind the beach, full of animals and quiet lakes. And the fat smoked eels, Maria! One day we would skip lunch just to have an eel, big around as your arm, and a half dozen Ahlbeck flounder." Max's enthusiasm for all of this is just like a boy's.

"Max, is food all you think about?" Maria just laughs at him.

The next evening they visit Elsa's place. While Maria was at work in her office, Max had made the rounds of the travel agencies, spoken with Elsa, and gotten a major, pleasant, surprise. Elsa gave him some traveling money. The money grew so much in his mind that he even brought back flyers for foreign travel, even cruises to Asia!

"At least you're giving the printers some business," laughs Elsa. She very much likes Maria, who strikes her as straightforward, quiet, and smart. Knowing that he's blessed, Max just has to give somebody a hug. He chooses Elsa, who has prepared them a small supper.

---

[1] This term, popular among the radical right, was used as to denigrate tastes and values that did not fit into their idea of what was properly German. Included would be everything from cohabiting without a marriage license to homosexuality, nonrepresentational painting, twelve-tone music, and jazz.

"Have you heard about Max's latest idea?," Maria asks. He wants to spend all of our travel money on smoked eels."

Max continues to chew mischievously on his rather smelly old pipe. It's giving him problems again, sounding like he's whistling for a dog that isn't around.

Elsa stares her brother full in the face, until he returns her look. Then she says slowly into his eyes, "Life is sometimes beautiful after all."

That evening it is decided: they are off to the heathland. With a pained sigh, Max bids a fond adieu to his seafood delicacies, as he decides that the coast, wonderful as it would be, isn't secluded enough.

"Which heaths, then?" asks Elsa?

"The ones near Hamburg, and then we'll see."

"Are you taking rucksacks and hiking?"

"Not exactly. Imagine Maria with a rucksack. Even the chickens would laugh at us. But her suitcase will be small, right Maria?"

Maria responds that beauty has its merits, and besides, they would be passing through small towns where, today, women will be quite passably dressed.

Elegance is no great problem for Max. He'll simply iron his trousers twice, and Klara will wash his three polo shirts. Then handkerchiefs, toothbrush, soap, comb, and he's all packed. He would even have room in his suitcase to stuff in some of Maria's splendid toiletries.

The week of waiting is slower than Max would have liked, but the joy, the desire to give the entire world a hug, holds on. He walks around as if he's won the lottery, holds pleasant conversations with all his siblings — even asking Jürgen how his friend is — discusses Peter's latest experiments, sits patiently for hours at his father's bedside (his gout having worsened again) and helps Klara with the dishes. But when 5:00 P.M. rolls around, he quickly disappears to pick up Maria at her office.

Nevertheless, he still has time to reflect on some bad luck he's seen. You see, he's gotten Peter back to work by trying to string him along with whatever bait he can find. Now, he has to ruminate about the bad luck. According to Peter, "This is shit. The mass is good, but it won't bond to the metal."

"Do you think the problem is that our press is too small, or maybe you haven't screwed it tight enough?"

No, Peter doesn't think that either of these is the problem. Still, they decide to work on this together. Max screws the press so tight that his knuckles swell up. They then leave it for two days to set. Still the same result.

76

Two disks lie there, one metal, the other one made of pressed material. Max is so angry; he smashes the whole thing onto the floor. Then, after a while, he picks them up and casts a critical eye on the pressed disk. Peter watches Max, thinking that he's lost his mind, as Max smashes the disk on the floor again. Max picks it up, examines it once again, and lets out a whistle. Taking the disk, he wanders into the kitchen, pulls some hand tools out of the pantry, lays the disk on the metal frame of the stove, and hits it with all his strength.

Shocked, Klara can only moan, "My beautiful, clean stove. What kind of nonsense are you up to this time!?" Max, though, is too busy to answer. Like a madman, he hits the disk and inspects it, over and over again. He takes scissors to the disk, even nails, but the surface is hard, too hard for delicate sound grooves.

As he returns to Peter, his brother is lamenting: "To hell with this. That was the fourteenth try."

"Calm down, old boy. Just record exactly how you made this, so that you don't forget what had to go into it. Do you hear: don't forget to write it down. We don't have to make phonographic records. It can be something else, too. Peter, I think you invented something."

"What do you mean?"

"I'm not sure yet, either, but try the experiment again, at least a dozen times. I tried to destroy the disk, but look at it. Come here and look at this! Not even a crack! Not a scratch! It's hard and tough! Do you get it?"

"I have no idea what you're getting at!"

"Neither do I! But I'm sure of one thing. If we can get this result twelve or more times, then the Deutsch family is back. I'm going on a trip now. While I'm gone, make twelve batches, and try to destroy them. Take a disk onto the street and let a car run over it. Make detailed calculations about how much it will cost to produce this stuff and how long it will take. If the experiments show what this disk here promises, then, Petey, you've invented the perfect molding material. But, it has to be cheap."

Peter pales from the shock of his own invention. "Max! Man oh man!," he cries. Mind you, this is Peter, the calm one of the family, who never gets worked up. "If it hadn't been for you, I never would have hit upon it."

"Stop it, Peter. If this turns out well — knock on wood! — I'll make sure to take my share. But first, we have to be sure that it is what we think it is."

"OK. Nothing like this ever occurred to me. I was just caught up in my disappointment in the fact that it wouldn't stick to the metal to make unbreakable records. The same thing's happened over and over: Böttcher tried to produce gold and invented porcelain instead."

"Well, if we wanted to make records, we might need to make this softer. Otherwise, though, we have a completely unbreakable pressed material. If this is cheap enough, there are no limits to what can be done with it. Think about the possibilities; electrical switches, telephone and radio cases, pens, cigarette holders, plates and cutlery, machines. Even really big things can be made from this stuff. My only concern is the presses needed to mold it. They won't be cheap. Still, I don't want to think about that until we are sure that we really have something."

So, as you can see, sometimes a bit of thought has a practical purpose. But the idea has to be found. Some people just seem to have ideas fly to them playfully. To others they never appear despite painstaking deliberations. So, here's the lesson: if a chance comes your way, take it!

"Tell me, Max," says Peter, "if this turns out to be something, what should we name it?"

"I'll think about that," answered Max in turn, "but let's not name the kid before it's born. When it's time to register this or apply for a patent, then we'll have time to think about it."

CHAPTER EIGHT

MAX ESCAPES INTO LOVE

A FAST TRAIN CARRIES TWO HAPPY PEOPLE, freed from the everyday. The door to their sorrows is locked, not to be reopened for ten days. Max sits facing Maria, beset by all kinds of concerns. Is her seat comfortable? At least he's wiped out the corner so that she won't be sitting in soot. She's going to avoid the corridor, where there's a stuck-up, military twit, staring in at her through the window.

"Bow wow," says Maria.

Max responds with a playful insult, and returns to his newspaper. Quickly, though, his cigarette burns a small hole through it, letting him spy on Maria.

Suddenly, with seeming seriousness, he turns and asks, "My dear Miss, do you have your Christmas tree already, too?"

Maria's only response is a spluttering laugh.

Shrugging her shoulders, a rather well-traveled lady asks her heavy-set husband, "How can anybody be so silly these days?"

Completely missing the point, he responds that "Henry Clay is closing his doors. Havana, goodbye."

"Sic transit Gloria mundi," tosses in a traveling salesman specializing in laundry detergent — the same detergent whose name is written on the skies on sunny days — and with this, his mind drifts back to the good old days, when he was still actively single.

As Maria and Max wink at each other, Max leans over to pass on a great secret, one of the many that they share. "I smoke herbs from the fields, woods, and meadows."

"I've noticed."

Maria turns to root around in her bag. It seems that she wasn't convinced that their travel money would stretch, because she pulls out enough cold cuts, boiled eggs, sausage, and ham to feed six people. As an encore: a big packet of cigarettes and several red-cheeked apples.

They eat breakfast, the best Max has ever had, including when Susi decked out the family table in delicacies.

This happy anticipation on the train. Max here. Maria there. Quite serious. The space between them is only for appearances. The two of them are completely one. Without a kiss or anything, still a tight pair.

Hamburg's train station spits them out onto the street. Is one a stranger in a strange city when one isn't alone? No. The train station, houses, streets, even the trees belong to the travelers. The people are good, so Max and Maria have smiles for them all. The unhappy see things differently, don't they? Nevertheless, our travelers don't want to stay in Hamburg too long.

"Maybe someday, when I can pay your way," says Max. "The cities are an expensive luxury. Expensive, but beautiful."

They go sightseeing, first the Chile House and other tall buildings; then it's off to the Alster to see people feeding the swans.[1] Finally, a mutual invitation to the Alster Pavilion for coffee. Then they hop onto a steamboat, which carries them past a few warehouses, in which the great, world famous Hamburg commerce has somewhat ground to a halt.

"I can't help but think" says Max "that everything here is as dead as it was during the war. I was here once before with my father."

"The ports are the bulwarks of the crisis. And the tariffs do the rest. The old trading families are crashing left and right. How can Hamburg prosper? Just a couple of months ago my firm was so happy to get a contract. We were going to ship our machines to Chile. But the importer wouldn't accept the conversion that the Reichsbank calculated. Mind you, that's where our salaries were coming from. Anyway, the importer wrote us he couldn't pay with gold, because the Chilean government would confiscate it, and he could only hope that we would have as much understanding for his position as he would have if the situation were reversed. He promised to try again, and eventually to honor his commitment, but he didn't know when this would happen. As a consequence we had to pay our wages and salaries in installments and shorten working hours for several weeks. If a company doesn't have any money, it can't afford to build up inventory. That's the way it seems to be going for German firms. High quality is in demand, but one also has to add duties, shipping and handling, and insurance. And revenues? A constant risk!"

"And then taxes and more taxes. A fine way to make money . . ., I must say. It's like playing the lottery. But Maria, don't rub it in. These are sore points for the Deutsch family. I haven't told you much about how things used to be for my family. We were quite well off. My father was a simple but very hard-working man who really built something. But business conditions and taxes ruined him about ten years ago now."

"And, can you believe it? Some people think that the bad times just started."

---

[1] The Alster Lake, in the city's center, is one of city's tourist and pedestrian meccas.

"That's such nonsense! Sure times are bad now, but it's far from the first time. They think they're the first to have experienced this, just like they think they've got the patent on German nationalism. The times just make me sick, if you'll excuse my phrase. It started in 1914. They said then that the war would be over in a quarter year. At least they were stabbing us in the front then. It was quite civilized: a bullet in the chest and you were dead. Now they want to strangle the life out of you an inch at a time. They even begrudge you the salt on your bread. Africa is bursting with salt, but the price here is so high because of taxes. I don't want to hear any promises, no matter who's talking. The only thing that will convince me of anything is accomplishments. As far as I'm concerned, we're still stuck in a war and only when everyone's completely worn down will they leave each other alone. At least that's something one can count on more than these sorry hopes based on conferences, meetings, committees, new men, and the desire to make things better.

But that, Maria, will be our last such conversation for ten days, won't it? We want to dream peace for ourselves and don't want to know what comes after."

"Shit in the pants, boy." Just at this moment — totally composed, right elbow on the railing, left hand on his hip — a brown-burned, wrinkled sailor threw in his opinion.

With classic Holstein calm and half-closed eyes, he stands there; pipe in his mouth like it has been there since he was in the cradle, he sets his glance on the broad, glittering Elbe River, running to the sea. Without a trace of fanaticism, his eyebrows slightly cocked, he adds that he certainly doesn't plan on jumping into the river.

Nobody knows what he's talking about, but certainly it seems to be clever.

"The old boy is right!" laughs Max.

They steam past giant ocean-going vessels, bobbing in the harbor, on which sailors of all colors, European and Asian, mop the decks, seemingly with a rough humor. Then, a joust breaks out. Two old salts, wet mops aloft, mount their comrades' shoulders like knights in shining armor.

Passing the Süllberg, Maria and Max jump onto the gangplank and soon thereafter make their way across the Elbe. As tide flows out, they see ships under full steam fighting the current on their way into harbor.

"The water is pulling!," a child shouts. That's right, little girl, it tugs outward into the wide, wide world. There's not much it doesn't know, and much of its wisdom is reflected in the eyes of the old seafarers.

That evening, after wandering with their small suitcases through the city to an inn near the Neugrabener Mill, Maria casts a critical eye at the Berlin rolls. Fresh enough, especially if accompanied by an egg and some ham and washed down with a glass of milk. Max would rather have a good old Ber-

81

liner Kindl or even a Dortmunder. But even he has to admit that the milk is tastier here than at home.

Now comes the question of where to stay. Unfortunately the inn, really a farm with a tavern, is full. You see, a traveling political speaker has booked it for a public discussion, and some visitors from surrounding villages are staying over as well.

They flee at the thought. "For God's sake, not politics again! I can't take it." Max runs his fingers through his hair comically, as if despairing.

Climbing the hill toward the mill, they are struck by the wonderful evening view. Max links arms with Maria. In the distance they hear the lowing of cows. The landscape is quiet.

"You are just like Bergner.[2] Any man would want to just pick you up and hold you. But, there's something serious about you, too."

Although this embarrasses Maria a little, she sees that Max is trying to make a compliment. Still, is this the best he can do? It doesn't fit with the landscape. She knows this is when she's supposed to hear violins, but she still has to tease him:

"Well Max, I hope for your sake that you're not leading the divine Garbo on, instead."

Then, after an awkward silence, "Shouldn't we find a place to sleep?"

The night begins with a hay ladder. With a gallant turn, Max offers to let Maria be the first to enter their "feudal" home.

"Oh, please. Men should always go up the stairs first."

Max, though, wants to be impolite, you see, he's afraid that Maria's not used to ladders, and just might fall down. The thought does occur to him, though, that if he only had a little spending money, this sweet girl wouldn't have to sleep in a hayloft.

"What are you thinking?" calls Maria from above, almost as if she can read his mind. "Even you can't conjure up a luxury hotel out of thin air."

They climb through the rafters, and Max shovels together all the hay from the first reaping, trying to make the softest bed that he can for the two of them.

"What if it burns?" whispers a suddenly nervous Maria.

"It's alright. We won't smoke." With this, Max calms her down, and they lay their jackets over the hay pile. "That's so it won't itch," adds Max, trying to sound like an expert. Maria hangs her summer dress on a pitchfork,

[2] Elizabeth Bergner was a major theater and film star of the period. She left Germany in 1933 when the Nazis came to power.

82

putting her shoes in front of "the door," as she says. In fact, it's the opening that the farmers throw the hay through. Then, in nothing but a shift, she throws herself on her rather odd bed and cries "Ow!" Hay straws immediately found their way into the skin behind her knees. They debate the question whether they should open up the suitcase to find the overnight things. "Absolutely not!, says Max, "then we're sure to lose something in the hay. It's like the beach: one'll never find it again."

But Max is restless: he stands at the little door and looks out at the stars from the entrance to their hive. Maria is lying behind him. What now?

"Don't you want to go to sleep, Max? I'm so tired."

"Yes, I'm just trying to see if the stars belong to Hanover, or Holstein, or maybe even the Hanseatic League. The accents here are so funny, so mixed up. And the night is so bright." All of this more softly, to himself. Hmmm, Maria is tired. That's good. Should he undress or shouldn't he? Wouldn't he look stupid jumping about in underwear, or showing off his socks with their holes? He glances back, to check if Maria can even see him. Stupid question. Of course she can see him in the diffuse light; he sees her too. How pale she is.

Stepping back, he throws himself onto the hay, just as he is, and lays his neck on his crossed arms. Far away there's some noise. Here there's only the cooing of a sleeping dove. The crackling hay smells of the fields. Propping himself up on his elbows, he peers forlornly across at Maria, looking like the Madonna herself. He can't help himself, as he reaches across to pull some hay out of her hair. Is it the light? He is so worried about Maria, how white her face is. His heart races and he touches her on the face with his fingertips, as if to test whether it is still warm.

Maria asks, with eyes closed, "Max, why aren't you sleeping?"

He takes her head carefully in his two hands and whispers, "Maria!" and lays his head on her shoulder.

A slight rustle breaks the silence of the barn.

Max feels a warm, soothing hand on his face.

"You see, it's because I am nothing, and have no hope!"

A long silence. Max thinks about the wonderful things the night could bring if everything were different. If the times weren't stronger than even love is.

Then, Maria whispers back, "but everything is OK between us, Max."

This is more than Max can take, and he pulls her toward himself so hard that it's almost painful, kisses her head, her hair, and runs his hand all up and down her shaking body. She seems so young. Then release, and a kind of almost unreal, godlike happiness clouding his eyes. "Stop, Max! This girl deserves your concentration." Breathing heavily, he lays her head on his arm and takes care that his hands don't stroke her body. Then, he forces himself to kiss her without further fantasies and decides that, nestled in each other's arms, they should now go to sleep. An Olympian thought. And it pays off a hundredfold, when again and again during the night he looks over and sees Maria's strangely smiling face. A child who nestles with him trustingly; a woman who smiles at him with deep understanding. A face that devotedly says "You" and yet is unspeakably pure.

It's a dewy dawn, under an emerald and turquoise sky above the black, steamy north German soil, with the cool sea breeze blowing in. They kiss each other happily and without a care. No shadows cloud their eyes, but their knowledge of one another is captured in them and beams out. They know they belong together, even if they haven't reached the ultimate unity.

A fountain pumps happily. Head under, little Maria, once, twice. Phew, phew, says Max cheekily, just wait, I'll give you a good washing! Thousands of drops shimmer in her black hair. She shakes her head. The thin material of her blouse reveals her pert, well-formed nipples.

"Alright, now. Time to get dressed." Max issues his orders. "Young lady, have you no shame? Temptation is forbidden; I'm going to have to arrest you!"

"Dear Mr. Max, could I please have an honest breakfast first? Then maybe I could acquaint you with this pump."

Now it's Maria's turn at the pump handle. Laughing, cheering, for now her Max is dripping from top to bottom. You see, dear reader, that's how division of labor is supposed to work.

Today they want to head out toward Stade.[3] Beyond it lies Hamburg's Kirschenland.[4] They would prefer to stay as close to the Elbe as possible; then they could smell the round elderberry bushes. The heaths would glow in a green like freshly painted window planters. Looking about, Maria is surprised about all the small hills and ditches.

"Humph. Hills and ditches! You really are sheltered, aren't you? Those are dikes!"

"Dikes so far from the water, Max? But the sea is many kilometers from here. I think that dikes are right by the sea's banks."

"But thinking is a matter of luck. First, the sea could decide to flood or break through the first series of dikes. Here not every day is as sunny as to-

---

[3] Stade is a small medieval town.

[4] Literally the Cherry Land, the Kirschenland is a relatively unpopulated natural area outside of Hamburg where many people go for recreation and vacation.

day is. Second, you saw how yesterday's tide moved up the Elbe. It too seeks its level. That's why there are ditches here, and dikes."

How it glistens, the Elbe. And even here she is broad, almost like the sea itself. Our pair wanders on and on along it, their little suitcases in their hands. They pass many people on the high road on which they now move through the countryside. The Elbe is no longer in sight. A happy huntsman, tall, blond, rifle slung across his shoulder, weathered cap on his head and a look of calm assuredness walks across their path. Tired, but not too tired to throw a "Guten Tag" their way. "Beautiful morning, isn't it? Had a good shot in the gray of the morning, a pretty girl walking along the path. This will be a good day."

Next come three sailors (sailors never seem to walk by themselves, do they?) along the path, wearing civilian clothes. Strange sight, sailors so far from the sea. They're like children whose parents have let them go to the circus alone. Rocking along on their unsure legs, they seem to want to gawk and laugh like children at all the unfamiliar sights, but their dignity won't allow that.

Max thinks that these days all sailors look like a mix of Skagerrak and Kiel.[5]

Finally they pass a young mother with a satchel full of brushwood gathered in the nearby woods.

In a small village they see an emaciated peasant sitting in front of a cottage slowly sinking into the moor. Even its window frames have shifted to an odd angle. As the Elbe moves, so the ground moves too. The man, still and contemplative, must be deep in thought. A female presence stands on a ladder beside him, long skirt hiked high, and scrubs the tumbledown cottage clean. If she had the money, she would surely paint the mortar between the building's stones white. No money, though, so a scrubbing it must be, as is the custom of the country. — And not only the custom of one country, for this virtue reaches all the way to Holland (or the other way around), only stopping on the Belgian border. — With every sharp brushstroke she imagines the face of the policeman who, this same day, led off — confiscated that is — their last cow from the barn. This is, so to speak, poor aim, or a misfire. The woman wants to take her brush and scratch the gendarme who, for her, is the sole embodiment of the power of the state.

The path leads our pair, Max and Maria of course, past a large, broken-down industrial plant in which feral cats are playing. Industry is in poor shape. Where there is no money, it seems that everything else of value falls

---

[5] Skagerrak is the name of the strait that separates Denmark from Norway and Sweden, while Kiel is an important Baltic port. The two taken together exemplify sailing on the Baltic.

apart quickly, too. From this standpoint, capitalism seems to be wearing a very sad face. One thinks: a man is successful and rich. Then, not much later, his creditors call his most impressive machinery nothing but scrap. His fine strong walls are nothing but a shack to be torn down and rebuilt. For years this plant kept the owner well, and his workers — well, not badly. Now — it's all dead, no use to anybody. The unemployed look back longingly and call the old days, when they earned as much in a day as they are lucky to get now in a week of unemployment insurance: golden. Somewhere the factory owner creeps away, not even beginning to grasp it. His wife's diamonds are seen as yellow and flecked with black in view of the glut. They will suffice, though, for them to live a few more months yet. Collapse. Collapse.

One sees that the mere will to dream of a peaceful world isn't enough. Life is staring us hard in the face from every angle.

The day comes to an end. Maria's feet are tired despite their frequent breaks. Then they are once again confronted with politics.

A troop of loud, slouching, young men wearing colorful uniforms cycle by. They are full of "the world belongs to us!" All are very young, full of loud debate. No question but that there are many unemployed among them. Nevertheless, one rarely finds such types among them who look as pale and hungry as the city poor, who don't have uniforms but can be found in ever-increasing numbers across Germany and especially in Berlin.

For Max the incident has an epilogue. Maria is shaken by bad memories. As much as Max tries to calm her down, it is useless. At first she can't take another step, and her face turns visibly greener.

They sit at the roadside. From not so far away the St. Cosmae Church Tower in Stade greets them. Max spouts whatever happy nonsense comes into his head in hopes that she will forget the incident. But it's no use until he refers back to it himself: "Don't let yourself be intimidated. I'm not impressed by them. And you will get over it soon too."

As the girl then continues to look just as pale and distressed as before, even though he has in the meantime been softly stroking her hands, arms, and hair, he simply takes her head in his hands and places it firmly on his shoulder, chewing contemplatively on a blade of grass as he does so.

A poet might write about how Maria's condition worsened at first. He would then have our pair spend a quiet night together after the long day, and all would be well again. But life isn't like that. It's totally unsentimental, has few uplifting moments, and, according to rules of its own, always moves in unexpected directions. It never shies away from showing us its favorite among unpleasant possibilities in order to test the strength of our affections. If it ever awakens a different impression, it's because we've put it there.

An atmosphere of improbability not only can lie over people, but also over cities. For example, if one were to visit the lovely small town of Stade, he would surely think that here there is still peace and quiet. Above its dreaming medieval walls, the old trees rustle and the mosquitoes whirr. At the café (near the gasworks. Parents send their coughing children here because somebody once said that they will then recover faster) the girls and boys sit, dipping their feet into the inner harbor and sing to the accompaniment of the accordion, North Germany's "national instrument":

> "In a Swedish herring boat at Altona, there asked a barmaid so fair,
> My sweet young one, may I ask you, have you space in your purse
> to spare?"

The old, distinguished houses bow; from the St. Wilhadi and St. Cosmae churches come pious sounds. At both the Swedish warehouse and in front of the wonderful old, rather ramshackle Hintze-House, young seamen sit with crossed legs and spit into the outgoing tide. On the Pottwärder, gabled houses in the lower Saxon style sit and dream in unending quiet, as geraniums hanging out of the windows give the air a lovely scent. Windowpanes gleam with the North German love of cleanliness.

Max takes this all in, breathing deeply, even though, hurried, he keeps losing his way in the narrow streets before finally finding an apothecary in the Hökerstrasse.

Max can't know that even in this little town, which lies there restfully, a fight for survival is taking place, that political opponents are squaring off, that an unemployed man had in desperation attacked the mayor, that troops from the various organizations had attacked each other in the streets, and that the harbor boats transport ever fewer goods from the town's trading houses to the large ships on the Elbe. Certainly the town shows a sentimental, sleepy face. Real life here, though, is just as hard as everywhere else, perhaps even crueler than in a big city. Stores go out of business, while the few survivors keep alert so that no competitors arise. Neighbors watch neighbors with ever-sharper eyes. For a native to go into nearby Hamburg and buy something cheaper than it could be bought at home, a piece of clothing for example, would never be forgiven. What little money there still is must stay in the town. That is the official line.

A young pharmacist looks curiously at Max, who tells her that Maria, "his wife," needs peace and quiet and wonders whether she has some medicine that would calm an upset stomach. The rather pretty young woman asks Max a few questions. Was something already wrong with his wife, or has she perhaps eaten something that didn't agree with her?

Max himself has already thought long and hard about this, and says politely, "Ma'am, my wife had a terrible fright, and I think that your good local milk turned sour in her stomach. Those of us from central Germany just aren't used to so much cream anymore. Then again, maybe it's the different water."

Perhaps Maria had never eaten ham before, either, thinks Max, but had only packed it in deference to him. The young lady gives Max a friendly smile and wishes his spouse a quick recovery. And Max leaves with four different medicines, medicines that produce a rather large hole in his already small treasury.

Returning to the small inn, he sees immediately that Maria's condition is even worse. He holds her head and brings her a bucket, water, and orders her not to drink. He then sprinkles her in the face, in his concern, so that it's as if she is going to swim away, all the while saying, "It's all better now, isn't it?!"

Maria nods her head in agreement and throws up.

Max is the kind of man who can only express his relief in such situations with great drama. He runs through the timbered room, throws open the windows, which open outward, swats at flies, and finally sits down on the bed to hold Maria's feverish hands.

At last Maria falls into a fitful sleep, from which one can see she is dreaming about being chased, but the word "Max!" comes up again and again. Max lies down beside her and arranges her as she was in the barn. From this moment on Maria seems to sleep more peacefully. In the middle of the night, an exhausted Max falls asleep as well.

The next morning Maria still looks so pale that Max seriously debates whether he should ask the pretty young pharmacist which doctor he might contact. Maria, though, will have none of it. All she wants is a cup of strong, black coffee — no breakfast, please. Max responds with a suggestion — but only if Maria thinks she can handle it — that rather than walking, they take a little cruise instead. Unfortunately, the heavens are also rather sad about Maria's trouble, and let a drizzle fall softly on the land.

Yes, a cruise seems like a good idea to Maria, too, but she wants to return to this town afterwards.

So it is. The city bus takes them through the suburbs of Stade to Brunshausen. There they sit, drink a second cup of black coffee, and wait for the *Jan Molsen*, an ocean steamer in miniature, that will carry them to Cuxhaven. Earlier, they had agreed to make such an excursion.

"What a great name, *Jan Molsen*. They all have such cute names here. And the fare to Cuxhaven is so low," says Maria.

"Isn't it? I've wondered about that myself. And on a four-deck steamer, too. Cellar, high tower, tea music, a dining room, everything your heart desires. If it had a tennis court and a swimming pool we could pretend we were really going somewhere. Look around, even the passengers are international. Hungary has eight representatives."

"Oh, Max," says Maria, laughing again now, "I think they're the musicians."

Two vessels sweep by the *Jan Molsen* in the shipping channel of the Elbe, one English and one Belgian. Cameras are deployed on all sides.

Thank God, Maria seems to be feeling much better. He does tell her, though, that he spent a day's ration on medicine.

Maria doesn't want to hear it, and cries, "Look, check out the little islands in the middle of the Elbe."

"Yes," groans Max, "they'd really be beautiful if we had a sailboat. Then we'd be able to land there and run around stark naked. But the sun would have to shine for that, like yesterday. Then, the Elbe would flow in and sweep away our boat. We'd have to stay on the island all alone."

"You have quite an active imagination," teases Maria.

The diesel engines rumble on. From behind the Helgoland steamer overtakes the *Jan Molsen*. The captain signals, and a friendly competition begins.

The fresh air and sea breeze invigorate Maria, who suggests that they do what all tourists do: write postcards. When Max begins to protest, Maria tells him he has no sense of family. At the very least he should tell them that he's still alive. They deserve that much.

"So that the others can envy me my good fortune in life," Max adds laconically.

Such is one of the quirks of the age. One feels embarrassed when things go a fraction better than they do for millions of others. But there is little sense in this powerful suppression of all affirmation of life, for renunciation would possibly mean still more unemployed.

They sit astern. The ship's flag flutters damply in the wind. Maria lovingly pens a greeting to her parents. Even Max has decided to write to Elsa and Peter. This in turn reminds him for the first time in four days of Peter's experiments, and he writes Peter a cautious question. Something inside tells him: Peter's invention is right on the money, Max, you can go ahead and talk about it.

Therefore he tells Maria about the only hope that the two brothers have in mind for the family Deutsch.

He puts his hand under the table and onto her knee.

"Maria, if this turns into something, would you like to be Frau Deutsch."

To his utter astonishment, she answers quickly: "I already feel like I'm your wife."

"Yes, I understand," responds Max, "you're a sweet, intelligent girl. But you know, that's also not the right thing these days, feeling like you're married without really being married. For a man it's certainly very practical and well and good that one doesn't rush into unhappiness for the rest of his life. Especially for young couples, who almost always, once they're hitched, grow apart as they grow older. But I believe it's different for girls: from every experience a speck of dust will stick to her reputation. A speck of dust, or, although she might not admit it, a thorn."

Maria says nothing, but her eyes begin to mist over.

After a while, Max continues: "Look, my sister Klara, for example, was a very pretty girl, and, I'm sure, no slut. It only took one guy to bring her to the point where she's totally through with life and negative about everything. My sister Elsa is the classic example of the single woman, and yet I think that she's sometimes desperate to take all her independence and chuck it out the window. You know, it seems to me that being a woman is like being in a predicament that may not have a solution."

As he says this, the *Jan Molsen* approaches Cuxhaven.

One of the biggest German ships, from one of the country's biggest shipping firms, is at the same time leaving the company's private dock. The giant ship is already heading out to sea. From the dock wave hundreds of those staying behind. According to old custom, the ship's band plays "Must I Then, Must I Then, Leave this Little Town?," thus tying today intimately to the world of years past. Just like twenty-five years ago, tears of emotion are shed. And great hopes are moored to the ship.

Our pair, though, walks through Cuxhaven in a bit of a fog. For a point of embarkation it is rather sober, though it's equipped with all the attractions of a port. As a seaside resort, too, it is quite peculiar by German standards. For exactly this reason, though, Cuxhaven has its own special attractions for some people. For example, it's not every day that one sees sea resorts where the sea washes up on broad, imposing lawns and slabs.

Max and Maria decide to walk out along the city's dikes toward Duhnen to enjoy their lunch.

After quite a respectable walk, and before their meal, the sea entices them. The weather and the sea make up for the soberness of the villages.

You see, the landscape and the Baltic are like the people who live there. All three seem on the outside to be cool and austere. But, beneath their surface, there is great depth. As puzzling as the sea floor, which swimmers walk on as if it's cotton batting, as mysterious as the jellyfish, which disguise themselves and are only visible when the sun hits the water just so, this is how puzzling the people are.

In their rented bathing suits, Maria and Max swim far out into the sea, until a whistle calls them back. Max, who exhausts himself somewhat doing the crawl, makes fun of Maria's breaststroke. His yell to her resounds:

"You swim like a grandmother!" Maria responds by turning her back on him and making out as if she is about to go under. The salty water bites her still-open eyes, and she touches — without really wanting to — the cottony bottom. Then fear seizes her, and she surfaces again quickly, only to find herself looking at and laughing right into the distraught face of Max, who has swum over to her.

Max bawls, "What do you think that you're doing? You scared me half to death!"

Making a face back at him, Maria responds that this is how grandmothers dive. Now Max gives an order, "Enough already. You're barely recovered! Come back!"

Maria isn't interested in stopping, and just makes fun of him: "Come back! Enough already! Don't swim so far away! You need to learn the crawl!"

Max can only admire this small person. "You look like you're better suited for housework than to swimming."

Swallowing seawater at this, she responds, "I've never darned a sock, but I can type all of your business correspondence."

"Alright, time to get out!" He gets out first to set a good example. "You know, Baltic water is like paprika. Now I feel like I could pull up trees."

"I know what you mean. I'm completely refreshed too."

Soon they are trotting, already dried off, through the quiet town. A crabber accosts them, offering by way of a song to sell them crabs. They buy a bag of "fine, fresh crabs" from the cart, and Max crouches in the sand, preparing them while Maria looks on.

"I got somethin' ta say ta yinz," Max apes in a singsong way the local dialect, "ain't no need fer the flags on the beach chairs; there're so many it looks ta me like they're at war or something.'"

"And leave your sorrows at home," sings Maria in response.

"Too bad it ain't that easy, little sweetie."

"Oh Max, so long as your watch isn't in the pawn shop, give it a look. I think we'd better head back to the *Jan Molsen*."

"Son of a gun: so much for lunch! Anyway, these would be better for dinner. Naturally they'll have to come along on the return trip to the *Jan Molsen*."

They reach it just as it's blowing its horn for departure.

Now back to the small town they started from. The *Jan Molsen* pitches, which is why there's a pilot on board. A wind comes up. The steamer begins to roll back and forth. Some of the passengers give Neptune his tribute. The Elbe is black, and now it starts to rain again. "This is awful, almost as bad as politics," curses Max. The Elbe gets more and more dismal and choppy. On the shore nothing but a few signal lights.

Late in the evening they land in Brunshausen just in time to catch the last bus.

Max longs for a Berlin newspaper and a hearty sandwich for dinner.

Maria, too tired even to eat, just wants to go straight to bed, but doesn't want Max to starve.

The inn's kitchen has already shut down. Max strikes out a bit beyond the embankment and finds the Island Restaurant. Wonderful place. Bacon and eggs for his stomach and a conservative newspaper for his brain. Inside the paper, a journalist and politician is accused — for the fiftieth time, no less — of selling off Posen to Poland. The title page itself shows the Reich Chancellor in Lausanne, shaking the hand of Poland's foreign minister.

As he returns to the room, Max finds Maria already deep in sleep. He thinks that this must be what a marriage of many years is like. The thought is almost grotesque: they've only been together for three nights. Still, the chastity between them is self-evident, as if it were that of an overly tired marriage.

Tonight Max can't get to sleep for a long time. He tries to force his thoughts away from Maria and tries to imagine the possibilities of Peter's material — whether it will hold, what it promises. The possibilities are almost endless. It occurs to him that he forgot to tell Peter to see if it remains stable when subjected to heat. If it does, it could be used for things in pubs and restaurants. It could even be used to make miners' and firefighters' helmets. He decides to drop Peter a note.

The night is short and bright. Our pair wakes very early in the morning. At coffee the innkeeper inquires what all they'd done the day before, and when he hears that they went swimming in the Baltic, he suggests that while they're still in Stade they swim from the bathhouse — which is right around the corner — through the meadows to the edge of the forest. That's a unique experience, he says. He then suggests another nice hiking route for them.

This is how they come to take their morning swim in a small, crystal-clear stream that in its way reminds one of the streams in Berlin's Spreewald. Swimming, they follow the meanderings of the brook through lush meadows to the woods and decide that since the innkeeper's first suggestion was good, they'll also follow his second.

Late morning finds our travelers again hiking through a flat landscape, but their hours-long effort is soon repaid in a most delightful way. They have already reached the vicinity of the stud farm in the middle of the woods that the innkeeper had described to them, and right after that they see the Forester Dobrock's house, secluded in idyllic beauty of a forest cabin. All around, on a broad mossy plain, beeches and oaks, between these firs and spruces. Among them are two gabled, checkered buildings with a big gated entry in the old style. In their tiny windows are window boxes filled with gardenias, fluttering in the wind. Hens cackle, and in between clean-looking little piglets run around the yard following their mother. Two somewhat tired automobiles are parked out front. A restaurant with checkered-cloth-bedecked tables stands in the background under the old trees.

Above all, the summer wind. The treetops rustle softly, silver threads in the air. A summer-fresh lassie leans heavily and longingly against a fence: Does Herr Ulf no longer ride through the countryside to pull her up onto his horse with him?[6]

Below, heath; above, balsam. Windblown gorse bushes and the light green of the birch trees like bridal veils. The landscape with its fragrance enters their limbs and makes them tired and submissive. Not for nothing are the places here given names like Silberberg and the German Olympus, not for nothing does it chime out in song: Take wing!

Language evaporates. Maria and Max hike hand in hand and in silence through the high heath. Here and there some wild creature skitters away. In the air the larks rejoice. Dragonflies glitter in the sun seductively. The ground blooms yellow, blue and red. Calyx and bees become one. Deep peace. A good German summer day.

As if out of nowhere, Max calls, "Smart, dear sister Elsa!, 'I see a colorful floor mat and throw myself down on it.' She wrote that in a poem."

With this, he throws himself into the field of wildflowers, pulls Maria to him, and kisses her passionately. Then comes their fulfillment.

"Such loveliness needs to be carried," thinks Max after some hours, and picks Maria up and carries her into the shadows. She is fresh and happy and indescribably more beautiful than before.

---

[6] This refers to a Danish folk song, translated by Johann Gottfried Herder as "Herr Oloff reitet so spät und weit," upon which J. W. von Goethe's famous poem, "Der Erlkönig" is based.

Pulling him towards her, she whispers with an air of mystery: "Now I have to make a confession."

"Oh God," thinks Max.

Almost doubling up with laughter, Maria whispers on: "Now we're going to eat some buttercake."

Max responds by whirling about and shouting up to the sun, "Now we're going eat buttercake until you explode."

Crazy kids, these, running back towards Dobrock.

"You! You!," he says, "now, let's act like we're horribly married. At coffee, we'll fight. Furthermore, just look at yourself. You think I'll show you to the others like that?"

He brushes the straw and wild blooms out of her hair as he sings her a song: "I am the Kaiser Maximilian. My bride none may dare look upon." He tousels her hair, which he's just brought back into some semblance of order. "You know, my little flower, I really wish I could just stick you in my pocket."

"Oh, so nobody could see me!"

"No, so that nobody could hurt you, you dumb Dora."

With this, Max purses his lips and whistles. Maria says that if he starts singing, she'll slap him silly.

"See there, you've already begun to learn something. My noble comportment is beginning to rub off on you."

They kept up this banter all the way to their buttercake. This so completely enraptured them and made them feel useless to all the world, that they decided to stand up the nice innkeeper in Stade so that they could enjoy the next morning on the Silberberg too.

"But would we then have to pay double the room cost?," asks Max.

"If so, we'll stay there a day less. Short but sweet," responds Maria.

In fact, the one day would turn into three heavenly days. "One shouldn't leave Olympus so soon after finding the way to it," is Maria's opinion. On the second day, they telephone Stade to say that they're not quite ready to return, and to please look after their luggage. Max throws Maria an astonished look as the innkeeper tells him through the old-fashioned earpiece that a telegram and fifty marks arrived, but that he wasn't allowed to receive the money.

Max covers up the mouthpiece and whispers to Maria.

"Have him read the telegram or tell what was in it."

"Do you know what it said, sir?"

"Of course. Just a moment, please. It said: 'I'm close. Think of names. It's coming together. Cheap, unbreakable, heat-resistant, tasteless, no smell. Advance enclosed. Greetings. Elsa'"

"The post office will surely hold the fifty marks for us; we're coming back tomorrow, Herr Innkeeper."

Typical Elsa. She wants to help make our vacation even nicer. She doesn't save anything for herself, she's not stingy, but doesn't have anything for herself.

"What a mensch!" Maria adds with some warmth.

"Now, Frau Deutsch. Peter is nice, too, because he's made the project work!"

Now Max is full of plans. "First we'll apply for a patent. Then we'll make the rounds of the major firms."

"Wow!" said Maria. "But if they are broke or don't want to help, I have an uncle who builds machines. Maybe he can help us."

"That's definitely worth a thought. Now, what should we name it?"

Thus an entire day goes by. That evening they call in a telegram to Stade for Berlin: "In Father's honor: PITTILIT!"

CHAPTER NINE

A SUMMER DAY COMES TO AN END

ALL SEARCHES MUST COME TO AN END. It's good, then, when they conclude as successfully as Maria's and Max's. Even the most peaceful of summer days will slip away, surviving only as a memory.

Our pair wanders in the area for a few more days, here and there, freed from the everyday. Then, Hamburg — and once again, life shows its normal side. First, they happen into a city district that is quite stirred up: just now, yet again, a bank has been held up for its payroll deposits.

"Do you think need caused it?," asked Max. "No. If someone's in need, they might steal another's wallet, even hit him on the head out of anger, or steal a sausage from a store. But you don't use a revolver to steal sixty thousand out of desperation. What shit!"

"You!," says Maria, "You're right. But aren't a lot of things senseless? For our time, today, so senseless? Think about the steaks and roasts that we got so cheap on our trip, and then compare the prices to what they charge in the cities. Are they not prices for those who make more than 400 marks? Simple people like us — with or without higher education — don't want to eat just soup meat and mutton. At the same time, we can't afford the more expensive stuff. But the stores would rather let the food rot than sell it for less. I mean, really, who can spend a mark or more these days on one veal cutlet?"

"Child," says Max, "at first glance I want to say that it's the middleman. But try to cut him out if you can. One mustn't forget that he has to cover the costs of distribution, shipping, train tariffs, and more taxes than I want to think about. That's why we could get thick creamy milk in the countryside for a quarter of what skim would cost back in Berlin. There's a surplus where things are produced. By the time things get to the customers, though, the prices are set. That's the way it is all over the world, and that's the way it is in Germany. Surplus here — shortage there. There aren't enough bridges. And only walls are being built."

Now the wheels are rolling again. From the train windows they continue to enjoy the tall grain and colorful fields of lupine. In between those are pastures with their heavy, black-spotted cattle grazing. Sixty pfennig to two marks sixty per pound in the stores. Here and there half-naked workers lie along the trainline eating a snack. The closer they get to Berlin, though, the more the picture changes.

The railroad embankments are covered in election propaganda, even though the campaign hasn't officially started yet. The unruly members of one especially large party haven't shied away from plastering any landscape, without regard, with their insignia and their demands. The other parties follow the rules more closely — or they don't have climbers who can paint the impossible parts of the walls.

Then comes a broad wasteland with street sign poles that have an exceedingly comic effect. To attract those who want to buy, but have no money, the whole field is festooned with slogan-covered flags. "Settle here!," "Land ready to build on!," Interest-free money for housing construction to eliminate the burden of interest!," "Big meeting this evening! Free bus ride there and back for anybody who's interested! Everybody is invited, especially housewives!" As far as the eye can see, not a tree, not a lake, not a street, not a train station, no provision for sewage. Around the perimeter nothing but fences.

Max swallows a curse and says bitterly, "Air, sun, houses for all! For all?" And so they roll on, towards the city where, in the meantime, so much has happened.

As soon as Max sets foot on the street where the family Deutsch lives, it seems very odd. Empty and quiet, as if swept clean, and on every corner policemen. In the stairwell behind the doors there is whispering.

A bit later he enters the front room where the three brothers sleep. Even though it's late, the beds are empty and the room is dark. But wait. What's that? A glaring light shines into the room. Max thinks that a car must have driven by. But no, it happens again.

Looking out the window, he's astounded to see police spotlights glaring up at the buildings on the street. At the same moment he hears Peter calling from the hallway, "Max, is that you?"

"Yeah, what's going on here?"

"Just a minute. First come back here."

In the back room, where the whole family — excluding Jürgen — is sitting, he learns that there have been street fights among S.A. men, Communists, and police.[1] Peter describes the barriers made of dumpsters and trashcans, and then tells him that it's even worse in the Rostock Strasse, where pedestrians now have to show identification. Police cars are constantly and almost noiselessly patrolling through the neighborhood. There's even an

---

[1] S.A. men, better known in English as Stormtroopers, were the Nazi Party's brown-shirted paramilitary fighters.

armored car with a machine gun stationed there. All gatherings in front of building doors are prohibited, but as soon as the police have shooed people away, they just congregate somewhere else. In the Birkenstrasse there's something of a Nazi cell in what's normally a Communist area. But today has been quiet, except for this ghostly driving up and down the street. The Communists and the cops think that the Stormtroopers are going to try an attack. The National Socialists, though, think that the Communists are going to try something. Nobody knows for sure. The workers are outraged at this Nazi invasion of their neighborhood. I'll tell you Max, one shot and we'll see the nastiest civil war you can imagine. But when you hear people talk, the neighbors, the people in the street — and remember, a lot of them are out of work — all they want is peace and quiet. They condemn this provocation in the strongest way."

"Of course! A civil war would just make everything even worse. Anyway, if we let these scoundrels take advantage of us, well, we can't just stand around looking on patiently like a flock of sheep. All we want is to be left alone and then they come and drag us back in. It makes me sick. Hey, where's Jürgen? Is he with them? Isn't two dead enough?"

"Please," says Elsa at this point, "sit down first, before you fall down: Jürgen's in Lausanne."

"You certainly have all sorts of surprises! I must say! How is that possible?"

"That's two questions at once: Firstly, he took the train. Secondly, he went with his friend, Paul Jones."

"Great. He's a loser, too. But come on. Do I have to drag the details out of you?"

"One day Paul Jones came by, really excited. We knew right away that it had to be something big. You know, he never comes by. Anyway, he explained that he was going to replace a reporter who'd taken sick. But the newspaper couldn't find out that the reporter was ill or that Paul Jones was going and reporting in his place. God only knows what moved that stupid little rag to send its own reporter."

"The reporter probably was afraid that if a real reporter replaced him for the trip, that would be the end of his job. It seems to me that he didn't have any special genius for reporting, otherwise he wouldn't have wangled the management that way. Jones thought that there would be enough money for the both of them if they arrange things well, and he took Jürgen along."

"Everything is crazy. Nothing can surprise me anymore," Max responds. "Children, I'm really tired. I'm going to my spot-lit bed. Peter, tomorrow let's you and me talk. Is everything going well?"

"Perfectly!"

"OK, then. Good night!"

"Max!," Klara cries out, "You don't want to sleep in the front, do you? What if they shoot through the window?"

"God, one can only die once, Klara, although I'm not at all ready to die right now. Children, here's something for you to chew on for the night: I have a fiancée and will, I hope, be able to marry her soon. Now, good night!"

Now he tiptoes into the small room where his father is sleeping. Pitt Deutsch now has many sleepless nights. Whether his gout is bothering him or it's just the times, it doesn't matter. He can barely sleep at all. Tonight is no different. He's lying, eyes open, in his closet-sized room off the kitchen, which has remained his separate quarters through all storms.

Max sits down by him and carefully takes his swollen hand in his own. The shadow of a smile crosses Pitt Deutsch's face.

"Now, my son, did you have a few nice days?" Pitt Deutsch is weak. His voice quavers.

"Yes, Father," answers Max.

"Nice of you, youngster, to come to look in on me. No one checks on me any more except Elsa. At most Peter, if he wants to know something."

"Oh, father, you mustn't take it so hard. They all think that they would have to make small talk, but their minds are really somewhere else."

"I know. That's the way the world is today. Sit down on the bed with me for a minute, Maxie."

Pitt Deutsch obviously wants his son to stay for a while longer. You see, Max and Elsa are his favorites. They'll listen to him without continuously interrupting him. And he knows he can speak his mind with them, too.

"Max, what do you make of what's going on outside?"

"Oh, Pitt" (when the children want to be nice, they call their father by his first name), "what can I say? It's always the same. Things aren't going to get better. We'll never pull together again. You know the saying about the good old Germans: four card players — five opinions."

"I know, but that really has to end, with everybody suffering. Barbed wire and barricaded streets in 1919, same in '21 and '23, and now it's the same thing all over again. The university's supposed to be closed again because of rioting, too.[2] There were problems when you three went there, too."

"Sure. I still remember that. Even then, in 1919, when for the first time after the war there was a memorial service for the war dead in the cathedral, the participants were shot at and had stones thrown at them. The police had to come with their machine guns to disperse the crowd. We just stuck our

[2] Nazi violence closed the University of Berlin on several occasions in 1932.

100

fists in our pockets and passed on the slogan: 'Don't react! Just march to the cathedral in closed ranks!' Among us were wives and mothers who had given a part of their lives to the Fatherland and who we wanted to honor, too. The service was hardly over, but when we went back out into the street, the stone-throwing started up again. I still remember it well, even though I was still only in school. Now nobody's going to just walk away with their fists in their pockets."

"Max, now you're getting all worked up. How can things improve if even level-headed people want to mix it up?"

"But Father, should we always just let ourselves be attacked? What, like it's wonderful today to be the golden mean. The buffer for both sides. Or more like a hydraulic press. Until all the air is forced out of us? If that's the way they want it, we'll just have two big parties with no middle way. Every-one'll have to go somewhere, because the press is squishing us out to the sides. This side and that side. It's still better than the splintering. Then we'll be able to go back to the middle when the pressure eases up again."

"It's already gone so far that people have had it with calmness and reason. Everybody wants to be some kind of radical."

"Now Father," teases Max, "but you don't want to be a radical, do you?"

"Me? Boy. I haven't ever believed that anybody has pure, unadulterated patriotism."

"That's too pessimistic, even for me."

After a few moments of silence, Max asks his father, "Don't you believe in the Kaiser anymore? Wouldn't you like to see him return?"

Pitt Deutsch doesn't need even a second for reflection. He answers quickly, "No!"

Max's silent astonishment forms a question mark.

"My boy, don't you see? He's been away too long and too far from the center of things to understand all of the confusion. Of course he can read the papers and hear reports, but he's living in an incredibly quiet country, a rich, clean country. And to understand what's going on here, you really have to be in the middle of everything. We can't let ourselves be ruled, anymore, by high-born people with easy childhoods and totally different ideas about life. That just won't do anymore. We've been a republic too long, and we've been in the middle of a disaster too long."

Max is amazed at his father and says:

"You're totally right, Pitt. The time to restore the Kaiserreich, if there was ever such a time, has come and gone. Somebody would've had to play that card a long time ago.

I'm just surprised that you've come to think so too."

"Boy, let me tell you something. I can barely follow what's going on now, and I'm in the middle of it. I can't believe that an outsider can come in and know what to do. This has nothing to do with my respect for the man.

But let me say one thing, Max: naming the new stuff PITTILIT is really nice of you. It's really rare these days that children do anything to honor their parents."

"Oh, stop it, Pitt. You're the father of it all. There's something else I want to say to you. I'd like your blessing for this, even though I'll do it anyway. If our PITTILIT succeeds, we won't be rich, but we'll have reason to be optimistic. Then, hopefully, we'll be done with poverty. And then, Pitt, I'm going to get married. She's Jewish. What do you have to say to that?"

"If she's a good, upright girl, Max? I've known a lot of people in my long, rambling life, and I've found myself with black sheep and with white sheep. The only thing I care about is whether somebody's good and honest. Everything else is secondary. We're all human."

"Yes, she's a good kid, Father. She's simple, straightforward, and hard-working, and she's very smart besides. She's just how I always imagined my wife. Right now she's working as a secretary for Kroll & Co. You've heard of them, they're a big exporting firm."

Pitt Deutsch asks his son why he's never brought her around before.

"I have to tell you, father, how I met her. She was being beaten up and insulted by four Nazis, and I got her out of there. I wanted to spare her any problems here in our house, especially from Jürgen. But I'll bring her by tomorrow. Then you can see for yourself what she's like."

As Max finally goes to bed, his siblings, still very much awake, decide to give him a good ribbing. "So you're going to bed only now, you beast! Just wait, though, we'll tell your fiancée just what a bad person you really are."

"Impossible!," Max calls back. He smiles and is thankful for his family, while they are thankful now that he's back home.

Not much later, somebody shoots at the police from one of the rooftops, and the cops shine their spotlights up and down the street. Max, though, can't be bothered. He sleeps with a constant, satisfied look on his face, dreaming of a future in which Peter Deutsch, Ph.D. (Chemistry), and Max Deutsch, Ph.D. (Political Science), own a small but profitable factory. Elsa becomes a purchaser there. And two small, charming children and their mother, Maria, also play a big role in his dream.

Peter, who's still unconvinced that sleeping here in the front while there's shooting outside is a good idea, rudely awakens Max:

"Max, listen. I think it would be better if we sleep in the hallway or in the girls' room. They're never going to stop their damned shooting!"

"Peter, just let them shoot," he mumbles half asleep. "We'll just build things up some other way. . . . But if it makes you feel any better, we can certainly sleep here on the floor. Then bullets will just fly over our heads."

He proceeds to roll onto the floor with all his bedclothes. With the words, "Stupid jerk!" he falls back asleep.

Peter takes up a station beside his sleeping brother and ponders whether he's the stupid jerk that Max meant.

Blind hatred rules the streets. Shots from ambushes threaten. Harsh search-lights scan the houses. On the rooftops, police search for hidden figures. Nobody can be sure who started things up again. — It is said that black-haired citizens were thrown from the night's final subway train while it went through the tunnels. — Rotary presses hum in the night: Impasse in Lausanne! Elections Influenced by Men in Party Uniform! Work — Don't Riot!

The presses roll furiously — the cops swing billy clubs. The paddy wagons roll into the courtyards. The first cyclists and airplanes get going. Another day dawns. One dead and more than a few wounded can be found both in the North and in Spandau. They'll only make it into the afternoon papers, in which there'll also be something about "New Hope in Lausanne."

CHAPTER TEN

LIFE HAS SO MANY ASPECTS

THE NEXT MORNING, her face tear-stained, Susi wakes Max while he was still in the middle of his most beautiful sleep.

Sitting on the side of his bed, she whispers heartbreakingly: "Oh, Max!," and again the tears start to flow down her crumpled face.

"What's wrong, little Susi? What kind of hopes have you had dashed? Even last night you seemed so quiet."

And now Max can learns the upsetting story of how Uncle Otto was arrested.

"Why?" asked an astonished Max, "Did he do some shady deals?" After all he's heard from Susi about her Otto, he can't imagine that.

"No!," Susi cries, "It has to do with the taxes. He was suddenly required to pay a tax that wasn't due yet. He'd been telling me about it, but I never got the details because it was too complicated. All I really understood is that he has to pay taxes that are too high for his current income."

"Then he should have filed an official objection."

"Yes, exactly, Max. He did that, and his case is still pending before the, I'm not sure what it's called, either the Finance or Revisions Bureau. He has expenses, you know? And they have to be deducted. So now they've decided, probably because they need tax revenue like never before, that maybe the expenses were for the business, but it's also possible that they went to cover the extravagances of his personal life, which they claimed would make sense given his station in life. Ergo, it was decided that he has to continue to pay his taxes at the old rate. Another appeal would be difficult because the expenses were for foreign travel."

"But Otto was never out of the country for long. Anyone who travels abroad for pleasure stays longer than three days. That alone should show that he was on business," objected Max.

"Of course he only took business trips. He was always happy to be home so he could be sure that nothing was going wrong. He hasn't taken a private trip in three years. He hasn't even allowed himself a vacation in three years. I got angry about that more than I want to think about. It's been a long time now since we've stopped going out; we hardly ever even eat in a cheap restaurant. For many months he has only drawn enough salary from the business for the most basic necessities, and the only luxury that he's allowed himself is supporting us. But now they say all that's not true, since anybody with his place in society has to be spending lots of money on himself."

"Doesn't he have a tax attorney? These days a businessman can't get along without that kind of help."

"Yes. He had one, but I don't know who. He knows a lot of attorneys. But the attorney should have done something to prevent this. There's no way they could just come and drag him off to jail."

"But Susi, please tell me how it came to an arrest."

Uh oh. Susi falls apart again and spits out between sobs: "Max, I can't tell you exactly. — — Otto — — Otto — — was just gone — he was supposed to pay — within so and so many hours — — and he didn't have the money — and when I called to set up something with him for 9:00 — the secretary said — she sounded pretty spiteful, too — that he had been arrested." This is followed by even more crying.

"The bad thing," says Max, "is that Otto is alone in his small firm. No one else to ask questions of. Could you ask the secretary or the buyer if they've informed the tax lawyer? Maybe this whole thing isn't even connected to taxes. Maybe it has to do with currency exchange and somebody is trying to hurt Otto by falsely denouncing him."

"I thought of that too, Max, and the secretary just gave the same kind of malicious answer, 'unfortunately I haven't been informed about that.'"

"Surely you at least know the names of the lawyers that Otto always mentioned?"

"A confused but hopeful look passed over Susi's face: "But what if the one we need isn't one of them?"

"He will be — and if not, then ask the last one you get in touch with for help, and then go see him. First things first, though. Wash your face with cold water and powder your nose. The way you look now, you won't get anywhere. I'm sure the lawyer was on a trip, or something else slowed things down."

"What if I don't see my Otto again?," Susi sobs yet again.

"God, Susi, he isn't a murderer, after all! How long do you think that they'll feed him for free if he hasn't broken any laws? They're probably looking for some kind of tax problem or something to do with currency exchange and just want a chance to go over his books in peace. I know that it's still unpleasant, but getting arrested is pretty common these days."

Thus comforted, our little Susi picks up the fight for her Otto with the tax authorities, without a clue that her beau will finally draw conclusions from her complete reliability and love and will decide to shed his principle of eternal bachelorhood. — —

Finally, after the third telephone call, Susi, nervous and sweating in the phone booth, hangs up and rushes to four addresses. This is much to the relief of the despairing people in line for the booth, who've even started to bang their fists on the glass door to hurry her up. Naturally, of course, the fourth address turns out to be the right one. Why isn't it ever the first one? Of course, it turns out that once again Max was right. The lawyer didn't know anything about it. In fact, he had just come back to town the day before from a business trip, otherwise he would have raised total hell. He was so mad that Susi was quite taken aback.

She had always imagined lawyers to be terribly learned, cool, and measured — and according to ideas she got from who knows where, also small, thin, and reservedly quiet — and now, right before her eyes, was a colossus with the friendliest eyes in the world. He wasn't particularly handsome, but supremely human, laughing resoundingly and slapping his thighs in rhythm. Just as Susi had earlier not been able to speak for her tears, the fat man finally pressed out, spluttering: "It must be a mistake — it must be a mistake."

Susi's heart swelled with pride as this man told her what a serious, hardworking businessman her Otto was. The lawyer then took a fat attaché case, gave Susi a long, serious look, and told her to come with him. He dragged her for hours through endless corridors and poorly ventilated government offices. Susi had never seen so much politeness in governmental offices as she saw given to this man. She kept stealing sidelong looks at him: how did he have so much in his head? He never even opened his attaché case, numbers and paragraphs just whirred out of him. At one point, he wrote a check in his very ornate handwriting, then recited entire laws off the top of his head. And every one of his colleagues whom they encountered in the corridors greeted him with questions about cases they were handling at the time. There was something almost miraculous about this for Susi. After four hours, she was able to fall into her Otto's arms. Generally he didn't like this. But today he squeezed her, even here in the strange surroundings, tightly to his breast.

"I'm finished for today," the fat man said, and suggested that the three of them drive in his car out to Hundekehle "to finally get something to eat." "But," he teased Susi, "don't tell the tax people. They'll claim that it's a five-star restaurant."

Now, back to the Deutsch abode. The still-crying Susi had barely left when Klara approaches Max. It would be pointless to take her problems to Peter, he wouldn't get it. That boy is so unworldly and takes all the jabs the world has to give him without complaint. No, he'd be pointless to ask for help.

"Maxim," she asks (she always alters one's name when she wants something), "Maxim, don't you want to go to the market with me?"

The unemployed PhD just gives an amused laugh. "Klara, my dear, are you going to buy so much that you need me to help you carry it?"

107

Klara presses on: "No, not that. I'm only going to buy what I have money for. But there's always some kind of problem there. No matter what, someone stops you. 'Do you want a couple of shoe laces?' and the boys look so bad. Oh Max, and the women are so aggressive nowadays. Just the other day one of them slugged one of the shoelace men in the chest, turned beet-red and started to scream, 'My husband's been unemployed for three years,' and then she just knocked the poor guy down. Last Friday the police tried to kick two men out of the market because they were selling soap without a permit and didn't want to pack up their vendor's tray. They then got re-bellious and started to yell at the cops, "All we want to do is make an honest living; you'd rather have us steal, wouldn't you? All we want is to eat a decent meal.' There was a long back-and-forth. The police tried to persuade them, but got fed up with the abuse and took them away. But that's not all. You should come with me to the market stalls, because it's worst of all there."

"Why, Klärchen? Do the unemployed steal things from the racks?"

"But where would they steal from, Maxim? They're quiet and depressed anyway. And how far would the get with such bulging pockets? And what could they even steal? Most of the stalls are only full of cheap cabbage any-way. But so many of the grocers are really nasty. You know the type: always the ones who stay in business just because people can't survive without food. They're really nice to the others, the ones who can afford to buy nice things. 'My dear Madam' this and 'My dear Madam' that. But those of us who are only able to buy a small quantity of even the most important things, well, we're treated like dirt. You'll see. I want you to tell Susi about the prices, too. Susi always says 'Cook vegetables once in a while, and why don't we ever have fruit and salad, why there aren't any greens in the soup? All that stuff must be cheap nowadays.' Today she wanted me to cook mushrooms. Last time I was at the market, they were 55 pfennigs per pound. Can you believe it, for fungus that just grows in the woods. For six of us, with the wastage, I'd have to buy three pounds, when really all I can afford are pota-toes, and then I need bacon or fat, and the little things too. This doesn't even count the cooking gas. So there's no meat, no soup, no fruit, and no salad. And where will I find the two marks I need for lunch? I really don't know how I'm going to stretch our money to get anything."

Klara's worn-out face looks even worse now than before. Max gets it now: this poor girl has had so little joy in her life, and now she's sacrificing what's left of her nerves trying to keep the household going. He gives her a loving pat on the shoulder and promises to go shopping with her; maybe his presence will make things, better. Then he tells her a little bit about PITTILIT.

"You know what, Klara, new strength always comes out of chaos. Why can't that happen with us, too? It will be good, I just know it. Now, how much can we spend today?"

108

"Five marks. But it has to go for breakfast, lunch, and dinner for Saturday and Sunday and Monday's breakfast, too."

"Hmmm, that's not really a princely sum, is it?"

They walk through the sun-dappled streets where the grocers' wagons are parked. Finally, the sun seems to have won out over the changeable, rainy weather that the summer began with, and the sun has shone down on the city for days now. The skies are a beautiful, southern blue. In fact, it's so warm that the houses seem to shimmer, and the asphalt softens in the heat.

Max squints up at the sky and says: "Just a little more rain and crops would be good this year. Then everything would be cheaper."

Klara laughs at him as if a little child had told a droll joke. She doesn't believe it anymore, and she should know. She's been in charge of the family's finances since 1923, even before mother died.

"Maxim, you're so naïve. If it's cold and rainy they say that nothing can ripen and that's why everything's so expensive. If it's hot and dry they say that everything ripens too fast at that heat and that's why it's so expensive. Just as expensive as five years ago, when incomes were considerably higher."

Their patience is tested at the first booth they stop by. Max and Klara are already there, when behind them a woman arrives who looks as if she's not used to doing her own shopping. Her clothes scream money from head to foot, matching her figure, which looks like it's treated to an hour of massage a day. She's every inch the lady in her pillbox hat, veil, expensive silk dress, monocle, silk stockings, and little snakeskin sandals. Her face is a wonderful painting. Standing behind her at a proper distance is her servant and chauffeur, holding a large shopping basket. What are Max and Klara compared to this vision? Klara, in her old housedress, bought off the rack for eight marks almost three years ago; Max in a shirt and trousers patches on his shoes. Yes, they are clean, but they have nothing else to recommend them.

"Is Madame being served?" affects the vegetable seller. You can be sure that she isn't referring to Klara.

This could take a while. Madame takes a raspberry and tastes it, demanding: "Pour them out. I want to see if they're dry on the bottom too. Hmmm. Enough. Much too expensive."

"But they're first class, Madame, fresh picked."

"Ten pounds!"

Next come strawberries, cherries, and Italian apples. The servant piles the basket high. The car is parked out front on the square. "Take these away, Egon, then come right back." Turning to the vegetable seller. "Do you have peppers? No? Why not? The tomatoes look too red, don't you have Dutch ones? Good, I want some of them. Finished? No, wait a minute. I want baby carrots, too. No, not those. Baby carrots! If you don't have them, we'll just move on.

So, Egon, there you are, in the meantime go over to Maier's and see if he has live tenches — wait a minute — and also Ostend flounder. — Are these wax beans good for pickling?"

"But of course, Madame."

"Good. You can send them along to me later."

"But of course, Madame. It would be a pleasure. How many would you like?"

Ah, finally this lovely customer shoves off.

"And you?" the vegetable lady asks Klara disdainfully. Max shifts his weight from one leg to the other. Klara considers the purchase. She will have one pound of peppers — they only cost 50 pfennigs — and then she can stretch them in preparing them. They look quite good, too, from up close. So, Klara makes her request. The vendor shovels them into the bag. No need to worry; they're just for poor people!

Max has a line, and this has just crossed it:

"You!," he says, "You! Don't just throw in the crummy ones from the back. Put in some of the big ones from up front, too."

"Ain't no choosing here, buddy!" the vegetable lady responds snottily.

"I want top-quality goods and not just broken pieces. Do you hear me?"

With the words, "Then go somewhere else!," the fat woman dumps the bag back into the bin.

Max grabs a large, pretty mushroom from the back, puts his hands in his pockets, and says: "I won't think of it. If you don't sell me good mushrooms right now, and not that junk from the back of the bin, I'm calling the cops."

"Touching da food's against da rules, understand? That's what I'll tell da cops, then youse gonna pay a fine so's you do understand!"

"— Excellent! And Madame who was just here, she'll have to pay a fine too."

"Emil! Emil!" the vegetable lady starts to scream, "get over here, this guy's getting cheeky! What a jerk!"

From the next stand over a voice calls out: "Fresh mushrooms, fresh, dry produce. Come and look at our wares!"

Max turns around: "If you really mean dry and fresh, then I'd like a pound!"

"But of course, Sir!"

"Some parsley, too," adds Klara.

"What a bunch! I'm callin' da cops on ya. Touchin' the goods, makin' trouble and then not buyin'. I'll show ya!," the voice from the other stand trails behind them.

Ah, one problem solved. With the butcher, though, a second pops up, as he adds a considerable amount of gristle and fat to the piece of meat Klara wants, to round the weight of a half-pound up to a pound. Here Max immediately turns on the cheeky Berlin attitude (especially as Klara has already whispered to him that the meat is suspiciously more expensive again): "Man," he says, "we said we wanted half a pound, not a pound. Put that gristle back where it came from. And how come the price suddenly went back up?"

This tone of voice always calms Berliners down. So it's no wonder that the butcher quietly packs away the extra and, using the same tone as Max, replies: "Don'tcha read the papers either? So you've got no clue about the new butchering tax."

Klara and Max give each other confused looks that quickly turn into grimaces. What's next? A margarine tax? A sugar tax? There's already a salt tax.

"Always on the most necessary items, always . . . — but, in the meantime Egon has to go make sure that the tench are still alive and that the flounder are really from Ostende. Oh Klara, you're absolutely right — I never thought that shopping would be such a trial. Every man should have to go with his wife sometimes."

Klara beams back at this: "At least there's one who recognizes it."

"The vegetable lady was pretty good, eh Klara? They were the same during the inflation, when I was still picking up the groceries, and during the war, too. Some things never change."

Klara thinks that Max could enjoy this kind of battle every market day, but she, well, she's tired of it. That's why the produce she brings home isn't always so good, and never what she wanted, just like today. "It's true, dear boy," she says to her brother, "I know I shouldn't just take what's given to me, when I'm having to count every penny. But I just don't have the nerves for this any more."

Such is our Klara: she takes care of the others, works out problems, often gets teased, is exhausted and joyless — and says quite simply that her nerves just aren't up to this anymore.

Susi, though, that cheerful soul, cries over her Otto as if she's going to burst at the seams, and has to be carried away.

Some days are rich. This evening, Father is supposed to meet Maria. Before then, though, there's so much going on. It's amazing how much can happen in just one day, isn't it? For example, a treaty is signed that many men have worked on for years. Now the German people will only have to pay three billion at the most, and then there will be no more war creditors.[1] It's just an average day of the year, a Saturday like any other. People are born, die, have

[1] This conversation would have taken place on July 9, 1932, the date of the signing of the Lausanne Treaty, which fixed the cost of German reparations from the First World War.

birthdays and problems (take Susi and Klara), but if all sides behave according to reason it can also be the beginning of the recovery of the German people.

And yet, the things that arouse the world on this day are small but have broad repercussions. Peculiar, isn't it, how fate knows to raise her warning hand when somebody thinks that he can overreach the gods. The great men of this world die in odd ways. For example, on this insignificant day alone, the flash of God made an international financier became a suicide and a fraud; on another, the brilliant arrogance of a great industrialist, who went to court to have reports about his factory prohibited, was dashed to pieces in an airplane crash near Otrokovice.[2] Two countries tremble. These two men, otherwise very different, had one thing in common: if whoever was less important than they and had to travel across half the world to meet them to do business were even a minute late, they would no longer be received. And now — there's all the time in the world! They were both sole rulers of their respective realms, each the sole possessor of their companies' deepest secrets. And now? — available!

In these same days the election campaign rages in all of its contradictions. It has never been as hate-filled and foul as it is now. An emergency decree shrinks and shortens unemployment benefits. Emergency funding is reduced even as new "crisis taxes" are raised. Besides this, workers' compensation benefits, pensions, and subventions for having children are lowered. Indeed, all governmental benefits are being cut once again. Mind you, these are benefits that the entitled have paid and saved for.

Various mothers send their young sons to the political party that provides the best food for its members, because they can't even give them a warm lunch anymore. Many of these boys go only grudgingly. But hunger is painful!

Politics gobbles up everything in sight: love, family life, joy, humor, and respect.

Those who, like Herr Deutsch, have nothing and yet still don't join the fray confront a chaos from which there is no escape. They see the best wills in the world dragged down, they see all the contradictions and no longer know what they should believe in. Over all of them, though, looms the peril out of which alone the strong will toward reason would have to grow.

It's only one day, and yet it is a day.

[2] On July 12, 1932, Toma Bata, owner of the Bata Shoe concern, died in an airplane crash.

CHAPTER ELEVEN

JÜRGEN FINDS SOMETHING IN LAUSANNE THAT HE DID NOT SEEK

G ERMANY'S POLITICAL VIOLENCE has claimed the lives of many over the
years, drop by drop. These drops are edging the country towards in-
sanity, just as drop after drop of ether falling on a particular spot on a person's head would do.

For the few who still have jobs, their incomes don't suffice even before
taxes. Those who are still working have as much anxiety about losing their
jobs as the others do about their poverty.

At this very moment in time two men, neither of whom is in possession of a
dark red press card, find themselves on a train traveling up and down the
heavenly-scented, blooming hillsides between Lausanne and Ouchy.

A radiant blue cloudless sky spans over the divine landscape like a glass
globe.

Halfway up, the train carries these men past the lovely, fanciful, and delicate village of Jordils, where better-born young girls are sent to be prepared
for "life," or, to put it rather differently, for what a small percentage of mankind thinks of as life. In Jordils's closed-off, flower-strewn cleanliness far
from any hint of dirt, there is no sense that in its sister town politics is decid-
ing the fate of millions upon millions of people.

If one thinks about it, this area seems to have a psychologically unpleasant shadow side vis-à-vis politics. In the presence of such rejoicing nature,
whose beauty words cannot express, how can anybody, even a politician, be
anything other than optimistic?

Ouchy sits upon Lake Geneva like lovely jewels about the throat of a fashionable lady, while Lausanne rests like a gleaming clasp in this same lady's
wavy hair. Close by, but not visible from here, on the western side of this
sickle-shaped lake, is the great rival to these two towns, the no less lovely but
quite bombastic city of Geneva. Here, so close to France, the Swiss element
does take a bit of a back seat. Somewhat to the east of Lausanne is the cheerful, small, but elegant city of Montreux, with its residential character suggesting a quiet place where the chosen few retire.

Lausanne and Geneva! Here, in close proximity just as the giants Mont Blanc and the Dent du Midi are to each other, convenes the thirty-fifth reparations conference. Here the talk is about mustard gas, bomber squadrons, gold reserves, and the dangers threatening the whole world. There the guiding words of the day are "compromise," "financial obligations" and "domestic politics."

The worthy representatives of the world press rush with their dark red press cards, those small pieces of paper that are the only thing that make them eligible to be given an audience, between the area's great, brilliantly-lit hotels, the Beau Rivage, the Schloß Hotel, the Palace, the castlelike Hotel du Chateau, and the Savoy. They sweat in narrow telephone booths, dictating their responsibility-laden articles through the ether.

They run and they hunt, sharpen pencils and make telephone calls. Each wants to be, indeed must be, the first whose telegram makes it out. Then they — each one of them having to process the thoughts of many statesmen — collapse into a leaden sleep.

As Lake Geneva shines, lit by a silvery moon, and in the distance, the beehive-like bustling, the ringing of streetcar bells and honking of car horns, drifts humming from across the water, white boats with gentle names like "Germaine" rock in the mild evening breeze, and cheerful lights shimmer from the shores.

The two men wander through the streets, bedecked with the flags of the six powers and pennants of the neutral host, toward the out-of-the-way harbor of Ouchy.

Here is the source from which the pseudo-journalist, dissolute count, actor and public speaker Paul Jones, with Jürgen Deutsch — his sidekick — gathers the day's news and dine, prix fixe of course, in a bourgeois, French restaurant that looks from the outside like a sailor's bar. Here rumors swirl about, long after they've been telegraphed abroad to all the important newspapers. It is here that Paul Jones, who, having no special press pass, lacks access to any place better, hunts for scraps and sends a report "come hell or high water" to his rag back home. The concoction that he brews from the gibberish he catches isn't always right, but it's certainly what the editors want the subscribers to read.

The little dockside restaurant is overfull today, so full that Jürgen and Paul are lucky to find space on a bench. The people are much more cheerful than they have been for a while.

"Did you see?" a rather English-looking man speaking poor French asks somebody else at his table, "MacDonald looks much healthier.

Tomorrow is the last session, but it's of no importance. Herriot was so happy that he hugged both a French woman and a German woman, too. It was especially clever of the Germans that they didn't just pick up their toys and go home at the end when they seemed to be so insulted. If they had, with their political shambles at home, they wouldn't have gotten away with only three billion. I just wonder if the preamble, with its "serious desire to build a new order in the world" will make any difference?"

"We'll just have to wait and see," answers his neighbor. "It's something to hope for. But remember, the complications will come from Germany's domestic politics. I'll bet you that tonight's and tomorrow's German papers will report that half of the Germans are happy and optimistic, and the other half want nothing to do with the 'Lausanne Pact,' and refuse to recognize it. Then all of this is just going to have to start all over again."

"But how?" responds the first. "The Germans can't keep demanding that we negotiate for years, again and again and in good faith, and then simply decide one day not to take us seriously. If they don't follow the treaty, this time more out of opposition than because of inability, and all this giving in and moderation goes to waste, I think there will be another war."

At a long table with benches sits a German, who eavesdropped with interest on this conversation, even though it was conducted rather quietly. He has a rather striking head set upon broad shoulders. His hands play nervously with one of the Berlin dailies.

Paul Jones, who had to strive mightily to refrain from heatedly entering the conversation himself, though he could only follow it with difficulty, whispers to Jürgen, "I know that head. I've seen a picture of it . . . heavy industry I think. If I could only remember who he is. He's someone we should go and talk to."

Paul Jones isn't far wrong. In fact one of the great men of poor Germany had taken the opportunity to escape from the hubbub of all the social activities to sit quietly with a glass of Neuchatel and think. You see, the rulers of the universe have cares in proportion to their power, just as the poor have to worry about getting their daily bread. There is, though, one small difference. For the poor man, suffering is something to be shared with a wife. Great men are regrettably alone in their suffering. Their wives aren't interested in knowing anything about their troubles.

This man, sitting quietly alone in a harbor café in Ouchy, his temples prematurely gray, his self-imposed calm betrayed only by his nervous hands, employs a good twelve thousand souls. If he can't keep his father's plant going, if he's not always on the lookout for new business opportunities, then twelve thousand more will be on the streets, dependent on the mercy of the welfare office.

This particular gentleman had joined forces with a few other gentlemen in a chess gambit — and now he was on the verge of losing the game if he didn't come up with a new, daring gambit at the last minute. In order to check a movement that was growing dangerous, he and his friends — political and economic puppet masters all — decided to strengthen a counter movement. The child, in the meantime, had grown up and was now be-

115

coming rebellious against its protectors. Indeed the child was — and it's always this way with children — neither as experienced nor as far sighted as its fathers. In fact, the child was under certain circumstances willing to use war to achieve its goals, something its fathers had unhappy experience of and wanted to avoid at all costs.[1]

The newspaper in our gentleman's hand was the mouthpiece of him and his friends. It warned the German delegation not to break up the negotiations abruptly or to push its demands too hard. Its warnings, happily, were heeded.

A great weight had fallen off of our gentleman's shoulders today. The next day, the stock exchange would be both more stable and more favorable for the first time in a long, long time. And everything will improve, if only domestic politics doesn't wreck things.

There was no need for Paul Jones to "chat up" this rather impressive man, for the two young Germans had already come to the older man's attention. The small pins that gave away their political persuasion hadn't escaped him either.

"One simply must do something for the young people," the man thinks to himself. "They've certainly begun to accumulate experience. Perhaps they can still be saved for a politics of reason." He points, smiling in a fatherly way, at both of Paul Jones's jacket pockets with the words "are you here for politics too?" He would rather have spoken with Jürgen, who has something more appealing about him as a human being. The pockets' contents, though, are not only characteristic for Jones, but also present a better conversation starter. With a broad gesture, Jones tries to say that as a "cautious man" he carries both left-wing and right-wing papers just out of pure interest.

"You already have a number of apostates in your party," responds the powerful man, tapping the badge affixed to Jones' jacket lapel almost as an afterthought. "A number of them are traveling around the country and not hiding their thoughts about what they're seeing. What do you think about that?" Without waiting for an answer, he turns to Jürgen and asks him a new question, "What are you at home? An officer?"

Jürgen feels very flattered that this imposing man with the many dueling scars, who may have been an old Corps student and a high-ranking officer, thinks that he is a military man. He doesn't want to respond with a bare-

[1] This rather delicate phrasing is Bergmann's attempt to say that big business fostered the Nazis to block the Communists, a move that, she felt, could turn on it rather quickly and painfully. Indeed, this would turn out to be the case only a few months later when Hitler and the Nazi Party came to power, and rather quickly outmaneuvered traditional conservative parties.

faced lie, but there must be something he can say to this man about his dreams. So he responds, "Unfortunately a shortened career. Impoverished family."

"Current profession?" the man responds quickly.

"Party member! Besides that, there are no jobs for us in Germany!"

"If one were to present itself? One that wasn't quite so military? What would you do then?"

"I would take it! Immediately and with great joy. Even the least offer, as long as it was enough to feed me. My family would be shocked!"

"And your party?," probed the gray man further. "You probably still have a great deal to learn. Life is more than field exercises!"

Jürgen is quite overcome. Indeed his cheeks are quite red. Somebody seems to believe in him for once. He has already tried so many things. Probably the things he failed in were not suited to his talents. Perhaps he'd wanted too much, like the time he thought it would be easy to start his life over again abroad. He hasn't been serious enough: his family is right about that. But if somebody were to really believe in him, well, no doubt, he wouldn't disappoint them. He still doesn't have a clue who the man in front of him is. But, why is he asking such questions? What does he want to know? Party? Oh, I see, Party.

"So, my young friend, why so pensive?" With this, the man brought him back to the present. "What do you think? You know, one can't serve two masters. One can only have small interests to complement the path he's chosen. Otherwise, each will always suffer from the other."

"People mature. And the Party by itself is not enough to bring fulfillment," Jürgen answers. "If I could stand on my own two feet, it would be high time for me to find a place for myself."

The three talk until late into the night; as they part, it is certain that Jürgen will have a comfortably paid entry-level position in this industrialist's factory. Also, a suitable position is opened for Paul Jones, albeit in a completely different region of Germany. While Jürgen will have to make it his duty to avoid politics, concentrate on his business responsibilities, and do nothing that would harm the interests of his new firm (exactly the opposite of what a party demands), a new page has turned for Paul Jones too. In the future he will have to demonstrate his abilities as an orator on a tour of public speeches in which he will be lobbying for a return to reason.

And so, we see how two men found a positive, and quite unexpected, solution to their problems in Lausanne. Not according to merit or ability, but rather according to fate. Isn't this like all of our lives in the years since 1914?

CHAPTER TWELVE

HERR DEUTSCH ONCE MORE CALLS HIMSELF TO ORDER, AND THEN THERE ARE MORE FLASHES OF LIGHTNING

ONCE MORE, OUR MAN PITT DEUTSCH wakes himself from his gouty stupor. Is it the feverish times that wake him up, or is it the odd circumstances that his neighbors have told him about, the trouble the civil servants have caused in the stairwell? This time, Max even wants to hold his father back. He says: "Just let it be. With a little luck we soon won't need it any more. I'm probably going to do the PITTILIT thing with Maria's uncle, who'll loan us the machinery. Just hold off a little while, we'll get by until then." But Pitt Deutsch isn't going to be held back anymore: "It's not enough," he says, "that we always had to help ourselves, that we had to sell and pawn everything, that the two girls are keeping us afloat — I'm not going to take their abuse after all the taxes I've paid in my life. Every citizen who shows respect should be treated with respect. I'm going to talk to the supervisor and see if he thinks I'm right."

What had happened? Oh, it's just another everyday occurrence. Because he wasn't getting unemployment benefits, Pitt applied for welfare benefits for himself, Klara, Peter, and Max. Admittedly, it was rather late for this. He waited until there was nothing left to sell or pawn. And now somebody from welfare had been there twice. Doing research. That would not have been bad and only right. The report could have simply said that the Deutsch family no longer has anything of value and is living under the most humble circumstances. More humble than some others who feel the saving blessing of welfare. But the welfare worker had made a mistake that didn't befit him. He had come by to see the Deutschs twice in a row without an appointment, and when nobody was home, he rang the doorbell of one of the Deutsch's four neighbors. This particular neighbor, unemployed for three and a half years and a Communist to boot, had a snappy answer to the question of where the Deutschs were. "How should I know? They're not sick, so why should they stay home?"

Unfortunately, the welfare man responded rather angrily, "What do these people think? We're not here only for them, you know." Perhaps he wasn't quite suited for this difficult profession.

He kept hurling insults for a while longer, until all the doors up to the fourth floor opened up to listen to him, behind which a good two-thirds of the inhabitants of this building were unemployed. The Communist, though, had answered: "You're wrong, buddy. Mos' certainly you're there for us, because if we had work, there'd be no welfare, and if there was no welfare, you'd be out of a job!" Then he slammed the door shut. And the man from the welfare office stormed out, down the stairs.

As soon as the Deutschs came home, their neighbors met them on the first floor and told them the whole story. "Just think of it, Herr Deutsch. He said that he'd come back on Monday, and if he didn't find anyone home, then he'd personally make sure that you don't get any support."

This started Pitt Deutsch's blood boiling.

He stayed home on Monday, then Tuesday, then Wednesday too. Finally he wanted some fresh air, because the welfare officer never came. So Pitt Deutsch went to the unemployment office to get the address of the welfare office that was responsible, and to ask whether what had happened was going to be allowed.

But there the man at the window treated him badly, too. Old Pitt Deutsch was so angry that he could feel his heart beating in his throat and his hands shaking, too. He forced himself to be calm, and said:

"Sir! I asked you a question politely and in a calm tone of voice. I have a right to demand a polite answer too then. Why do you talk to me like this? I may have no job, no money, but I'm still your equal. I want to see your supervisor. Let him know I'm here."

This man tried to fob off our Pitt Deutsch with the reply, "He's not here!" So he just said: "Then I'll wait. Sooner or later he has to come back."

He sits and waits, and waits, and hundreds of others are waiting with him. They're icily silent. And the air feels like it could explode. He waits for an hour, two hours. Time is money. But if you don't have money, you at least have time. Finally the supervisor shows up. He was probably there the whole time. Only nobody told him that Herr Deutsch wanted to speak with him.

The supervisor is a completely different type. He's polite and has a sympathetic, human tone of voice, too. Explaining his concern to this man in itself takes away half of Pitt's outrage.

"I completely understand Herr Deutsch. I'm sorry to say too, though, that — and you need to understand this — these days people are all so worked up. The clients who walk through the door aren't always so sweet with us, either. We're supposed to cut back, economize, reduce costs, and yet we can see with our own eyes just how desperately people need this little bit of money."

"I know. I know," Pitt Deutsch responds shyly, "I understand all that. I know that the waves can get rough sometimes here. But we need oil on the water to calm the seas down. Yeah, oil. When are we going to see some oil?"

The supervisor doesn't know, either, but he tells Pitt the name of his colleague at the welfare office whom Pitt should turn to and trust.

Even here, a few streets over, Pitt Deutsch, after cooling his heels for a couple of hours, is treated with the utmost courtesy. All he wants is to lodge a complaint against the official who visited his building and his conduct in the stairwell, and to request another visit at a time when he would be home.

He is asked to go home and wait. Unquestionably somebody would be by today. Contented, Pitt Deutsch goes home and waits. Klara, Peter, and Max wait with him. Max even declines to pick Maria up, hoping secretly that she'll come by to see him of her own accord. Maria does show up, and so does Elsa, who, to be on the safe side, has just cancelled the lease on her small apartment, although Max thinks that this is unnecessary. She's in the process of giving up everything that she's worked so hard for. The only person who doesn't come is the promised welfare official.

They sit around and wait until late in the evening, then all day again, for two weeks. Nobody from welfare bothers to show up. Max joins in the waiting because he wants to be sure that the elections have an impact on his plans.

"I don't want to," he says, "build something up with hard work, go into debt, and put forth my ideas if the state won't give me a small guarantee — though such guarantees don't amount to much these days in any case — that it won't destroy everything before it's even built. I just refuse! I'm waiting, too."

One day, out of nowhere it seems, the Litfass poles on the corners are almost virginally clean, standing about without a sign of politics.

On the corner near the Deutsch's flat the fat, round, Berlin "auntie" stands, enjoying the sunshine, wearing a white and green checkered dress with no trace of printer's black. That's never been the case before. Perhaps too much black ink has flowed already? Perhaps all the rising and sinking rollers of the rotary presses have exhausted the supply of red and black ink? Is private life dead, too, so that it no longer calls people to the movie theater or even to have a soft drink of brand X?

121

One old woman — careworn and fat — for whom most people would use the harsh expression "nervous pig,"[1] stands in the middle of the boulevard, paying no heed to traffic laws or to traffic itself. All alone, wide grin on her face, she stares, grinning, at the advertising pillar until another woman comes by, at which point she stops, folds her hands across her belly, and enjoys herself with typical Berlin humor, half talking to the other: "Cleanliness is next to godliness. It does my heart good."

It's only been a few days since then, but it feels like a long time.

Pitt and his children still don't believe in the calm period that is supposed to begin. Even though such a period really was supposed to come, because the German people have already decided.

Max certainly has his opinion. "Some parties will again rest on the laurels of their successes, until others take control from them," thinks Max. "Whichever ones want to survive this will have to be tremendously careful."

On the whole, though, he's thinking less about politics than about himself. It was right after the latest round of elections that he turned his full, feverish attention to finding uses for PITTILIT. He doesn't want to let renewed unrest of a purely political kind slow him down any longer. All he really wants is to be able to turn his full attention to work, which is demanding much more of him now, requiring all his powers if he's going to pull his family out of its misery. Well, if he wanders into the middle of a tumult on the street, like has happened to a few people who were passing by, or if he has to look at injustice at a too-close distance, like back then with Maria, that's one thing: he'll join in and fight for what he's decided is moral and right. He wouldn't have had it any other way, because like Father says, this short life's nothing but toil and struggle. And as Peter thinks — and he agrees — if you avoid these fights then your very life is pointless. Other than this, though, he wants nothing more than quiet and enough energy for *his* return to prosperity. Max is a man who thinks that egoism is something very healthy. Despite the hungry years and . . . bad times, he still believes that a man can't put his faith in a party, thinking that it will see to it that he won't be allowed to starve. If somebody has a chance to take a job, well he should, even if it's not what he was trained for. He should do nothing else but work hard for himself alone, because that's the best way to help others too.

In any case, even without work Max was too mentally active to be driven by the mental desperation — which is the most dangerous thing for the

---

[1] The original German refers to the woman as "Kummerspeck," which is a slang term for somebody who puts on a lot of weight because of nervous overeating.

unemployed — to seek refuge in either harmless pastimes or politics. In contrast to many of his fellow countrymen, he didn't think that it was stupid ignorance to avoid political engagement. On the contrary, he thinks that political leaders must find it a lot easier to pull the dull, the blunted, and the narrow-minded into their orbit than it is to capture people who are capable of wrestling with their mental anguish themselves.[2]

Maybe they'll call him ignorant, especially now when all he wants to think about is work. Maybe they'll despise him because he won't let politics rule his life. His contempt for the struggle of brother against brother, though, is greater than theirs for him.

Max develops the same single-minded interest for his and his family's private life that others have for politics. Sometimes he ponders the fact that the biggest haters are those who still find themselves in protected positions.

He wonders, too, why, as he always has to be reminded, people seem to remember the inflation, but not the war. When people speak of the sins of the past, it always rings in his ears: and the inflation? Somebody is always saying: I lost all my money, I was swindled out of all my hard-earned savings. — But the silver-haired mothers, the girlfriends, and the wives; well, they stay quiet, thinking: they've unfortunately forgotten that our flesh and blood, indeed, our everything, was taken away!

Max takes stock of his situation. Is desperation going to get the best of him now, just when things are getting better again? Is he going down the same road as Peter did? Is he going to lose his faith in humanity? Is money what they care about most? Do human flesh and blood count for nothing? "No, no, and always no!" comes the cry from his soul. "I refuse to believe that man is evil. He's at his wit's end, pulled in all directions, confused, but he's fundamentally good!"

Using humanity's strongest weapon, the belief that the human being is good, Max returns to his task, and it is like a cheerful, honest young girl who with her lively greeting calls forth a friendly answer.

He shops Peter's PITTILIT around from firm to firm, and doesn't lose hope when they send him down the road or dither in the most bureaucratic, unhelpful way. Then, finally, Maria's uncle turns out to be the man who has faith in him and in the project. With the requisite headaches, financial commitments, debts, and a lot of mutual trust, the project finally gets off the ground. Maria's uncle lends the form presses. Susi brings the good news that her fiancé has twenty thousand marks he wants to invest. The head man, Dr. Max Deutsch, cuts a very good deal — one that he's quite proud of — with

---

[2] The German word in the text for political leaders is *Führern,* which would certainly remind the readership of Adolf Hitler, who very self consciously styled himself "Der Führer," the leader.

123

a third man, a property owner who has a storage facility that's been empty for who knows how long. In order to keep the young firm from crashing under debt before it even starts production, the rent is set as a percentage of the profits.

"If we do well," Max explains to his relatives, both old and new, "then our landlord will do well, too. No harm, and certainly better than if we saddle ourselves with debt before we turn a profit."

The first thing this dear, foolish man, our Max, did, was schlep, arms straining, the old heavy copy press, "WITH GOD!," from the cellar into his new office, well outfitted with furniture from defunct firms. Everybody who went into Max's office was warned not to make light of the old machine, because for Max it was not a joke at all. Nor for Peter. In fact, the latter took it upon himself to coat the press with pure, transparent, amber-colored shellac, even though lubricating oil would be more beneficial to it.

The family Deutsch — especially Pitt — the family Sommer, and the other silent partners of the enterprise think that this new beginning demands a celebration, even if it is rather muted and suited to the times. Such occasions need to be marked.

Max, though, voices his opposition. "There will be plenty of time later to celebrate," he says.

"The young man is just like me!," thinks an astonished Pitt Deutsch, who is rejuvenated and more than ready to get back to work and in some areas gives very worthwhile tips. But then he uses his paternal authority to outvote Max.

"You know," he says, "I always put off the joyful things in my life and that just wasn't right. Whatever you can say about Martha, my wife, well, she didn't have it easy with me. She wanted so much to laugh, go out, and go dancing, even. She was so pretty and full of life when I married her. And so hard-working, too. But I never had any time or feel for any of that. That's why she was so sullen at the end. She got so little out of life, my Martha. — Now, boy, come on. Don't be like me in that regard. Come on and have a glass of beer with us."

After a long discussion, they all decide that the celebration will be combined with an excursion. These days, with a large family, this runs into quite a lot of money.

So Pitt, his family, and his new family, including Otto, Susi's freshly baked fiancé, make a trip into the country one Saturday, feeling jovial, friendly, and just a little bit proud of themselves. (Just yesterday the representative from the Welfare Department came by, and they told him they no longer needed him.) This time they head west.

The old people are quite surprised by what they see. "My God, how every-thing's changed." There's a film studio where there was a hunting lodge just yesterday. Look, tents and little wooden houses where five years ago "the foxes said goodnight." "But look at this mess. Sandwich wrappers thrown into the woods, just like they used to be. This is just scandalous," com-plained a rather peeved Pitt Deutsch.

Klara schleps a rather large package along, and, after fielding a lot of questions about it, tells the group she has sandwiches for everyone.

Max, who was already looking forward to a Holsteiner schnitzel — to-day, damn the cost — looks at her despairingly and could almost hug and kiss his future brother-in-law when he says with quiet emphasis, "The sand-wiches are just a little extra snack."

In his quiet way, Peter asks his brother Max, almost as an aside, if all the engagements should be celebrated today. At this, Max looks just at him just as dumbfoundedly as Peter had looked at Max when they discovered PITTILIT. Then he cries out, "Boy, that's a great idea! Why didn't I think of that?"

And so, in complete harmony, the whole family wanders off to an out-door restaurant, the kind with a cover charge.

But this was strange. — — What was going on here? — — Had time stood still? Was it running backwards? Or was it like a dog running in circles chasing its tail? Even Herr Pitt Deutsch said, "Children, pinch me. It's as if Martha's still alive."

Somewhere outside there was terror, and half the German population (may-be more) was suffering unspeakably. But here sat — — not exactly capital-ists, no, far from it — — but middle-class Germans who still had secure jobs, in their Sunday best. Perhaps they're not as joyous as they once were, but, then again, Prussians have never been a demonstrative lot.

No empty seats here, and from the dance floor, where to the strains of the Fridericus March young men were leading their girls before them, the Viennese wooden chairs were migrating to the garden to give assistance. The sweating waiters carried beer upon beer, coffee upon coffee. Over there, in the glass pavilion a salon band, sax player included, struck up pre-war songs from the Rhineland.

Right in the middle of the large garden, wearing civilian clothes — re-minding us that the past is really past — stood a colleague of the long-dead Maxe Graf, a military musician who conducted the "Entrance of the Gladi-ators" exactly as he would have twenty years ago, followed by the Trouba-dour and then the most famous tunes from *Carmen*. Women, carefully dressed up and without makeup, most of them with their hair up in a bun, sang along — each and every one of them cigar makers.[3] Little children, many in sailor suits, ran among the chairs and begged their parents for a penny for candy from the machine, for a lantern to carry, or for a swing in the air.

The men left the women they came with and played skat and other card games. In the large hall, a "modern" quilt made of paper roses was spread out. The girls twirled in long skirts of muslin and organdy that whipped up clouds of dust (how the crowd cursed that!). And between the strains of the saxophone and clarinet a "dance master" called out the steps.

Then the new youth stormed overheatedly into the garden's evening darkness, arriving fresh from their ten-minute train ride from the nation's capital. Nothing different about them from their predecessors of 1913; they're here for the fireworks show across the lake.

Fire then shot into the sky and glowing snakes walked on the water. What these youth of 1932 really liked, though, were the loud "cannon shots" and the almost invisible "jumping jacks," not to mention the spinning fire wheels. An exploding zeppelin flew through the air on a wire. Even higher in the sky than this small imitation of aeronautics two airplanes circled, dragging lighted advertising signs behind them. Before anybody could even look at them, though, magnesium fire burned, giving a ghostly glow to the lake and the woods.

The masses let out an "Ah!" and "Oh!" at the green and the red and the gold rain.

Over on the other shore of the lake, unfortunately, an outfit of police, once known as security police, aka protection, was also illuminated.[4] They had the thankless task of keeping all those who couldn't pay the fifty pfennig price of admission from enjoying the event at close range.

But then the last artificial star burned out. The satisfied citizens headed for home, colliding with the throngs who now were allowed to enter without paying.

---

[3] *Carmen* (1875), by Georges Bizet, is a tragic opera whose title character is a poor cigar maker in Seville.

[4] Bergmann contrasts the terms "Schupo," "Sipo," and "Schutzmann" here, seemingly using the different connotations of the terms to subtly comment on the use of police to keep the poor down and under control. Schupos, or Schutzpolizei, were ordinary uniformed police officers. Sipos, or Sicherheitspolizei, were paramilitary police who were active in the Weimar Republic's early days, and were especially noteworthy for quelling revolutionary activity. Schutzmann is an old term for police, but has the literal meaning of "man who protects," and is thus translated here as "protection."